Never Going Back

NIA

To: Patricia
Stay Beautiful!
Nia ♡
'15

ISBN: 10:

1522919201

ISBN-13 978-1522919209

CONTENTS

CONTENTS

ACKNOWLEDGMENTS

Giving honor and thanks to the man above. Thanks to all of my friends, family, and loved ones for supporting me. Thanks to everyone who is reading this book.

Chapter 1

Briana

Not Gonna Cry

Speeding down the highway with singer Ashanti's song "Rain On Me" blasted as loud as it could go. The DJ on the radio picked the perfect song to play because it was exactly how she was feeling. Her heart was racing, her hands were gripping the steering wheel, and her adrenaline was on high. She was speeding down the highway going 80 mph in a 55 mph speed zone.

She slightly cracked the car window open to allow some of the cool Minnesota fall air blow into the car and onto her. She needed to cool off because right now she is hot with anger, and driving with no destination. She can't believe she is in this mess again. Why hadn't she learned the first time.

She was desperately trying to think of somewhere to go. She felt a surge of anger rush through her body. *I can't go home shit!* She thinks to herself while banging her fist on the steering wheel. She reaches to pick up her cell phone to try to find somebody to call.

The screen lights up flashing a picture of her and him. He was calling her again for the third time in the past 10 minutes. Right now she hated that picture of them, and wished she had never saved it as the caller id picture for his number. Rolling her eyes, she swiped the screen to ignore the call.

She felt another surge of anger rush through her body making her feel like she wanted to scream. One of those screams that you hear in a scary movie. The kind of scream that's loud, high pitched, and ear piercing. She felt like screaming would make her feel better right now. At least a good scream would help her release some of the frustration and anger she was feeling.

She decided against the scream. It was so unlike her. She focused on the road and started to sing along with the Ashanti song. *Lord won't you take this pain from me….*

She took a deep breath and let it out slow. She felt her body relax a little so she took another deep breath and let it out slow. Anger and emotion are consuming her mind and she knows that she needs to relax so she can get her thoughts together.

She looked at her phone. That jerk had the nerve to be calling again. She sucked her teeth and let the phone ring until it went to voicemail.

Every time he called; she became angrier. His calling was

truly pissing her off. Sending flash backs through her mind of the whole scene that put her in the car and out on the highway trying to figure out where to go in the middle of the night.

What pisses her off the most is that he had the nerve to be calling her over and over again after the situation that just went down. Like the two of them really had something to talk about. At this very moment she hated him more than ever. In her mind he is a jerk, and a dumb ass, and he deserves to be locked up somewhere in solitary confinement.

Everything in her wanted to go back to where she left him and blow the fucking place up with him in it. She knew she couldn't do that. Because then she would be locked up somewhere in solitary confinement and he wasn't worth all that.

She looked around her. It was dark outside and not a car in site. She slowed down her speed a little just in case a police car was hiding out underneath a bridge setting up a speed trap. The last thing she needs is a speeding ticket to add to her stress.

The radio DJ came on the air saying that was some old school Ashanti that he just played. *Old?* She said out loud. Seemed to her like that song just came out not that long ago. The DJ played another song he called old school. How You Gonna Act Like That by Tyrese. That song allowed her to get lost in the music for a moment and forget about her situation.

Reality resurfaced when she saw her phone screen started flashing again. The screen was only flashing without ringing because she turned the ringer on silent when he started his phone call rampage.

She looked at the phone and saw the picture of them again. "I hate you" She said out loud. She never liked using that word because she was taught that "Hate" is a strong word. But right now that is how she truly felt, because her body is aching, her head is throbbing, her mouth is dry, and she is driving down the highway in the middle of the night with nowhere to go. All because of his dumb ass.

Her phone lit up again and she ignored the call. She thought to herself *What the fuck is his problem? Doesn't he understand that he fucked up?* She set the phone on the passenger seat and continued to drive. *No he couldn't understand that because he is crazy.* She thought to herself.

She knew that she needed to stop somewhere just to get her thoughts together. She saw a sign that said there was a gas station coming up at the next exit. She decided that she would go there. At least that would be somewhere safe to chill out for a moment until she could figure out who to call.

She took her foot off of the gas slowing her speed down. She turned the radio down to a lower volume, clicked on the blinker to signal she was switching lanes, and got off the highway at the exit.

She pulled her black Nissan Altima into the gas station and parked. There wasn't a soul in sight. Her car was the only car out there in what looked like a ghost town. It was the middle of the night and it seemed like she was the only person outside except for the lonely cashier who had the pleasure of working the graveyard shift.

The song on the radio switched to a Mary J Blige hit "Not Gon' Cry." It was like whoever the DJ was that night was feeling her pain. They were playing all the songs that were related to her situation right now. The radio DJ's choice of music was speaking to her heart.

At this very moment she felt like she didn't want to cry. Not for him. Not again. To her it felt like she could hear the lyrics clearer right now than she had ever heard them before and she had heard the song a million times.

She looked at herself in the visor mirror. Touching the bruises that he left again. On her face, on her chest, and on her arms. Her lip was busted, her hair was wild, her clothes were ripped, she was missing one earring, and her hand was throbbing.

Her reflection was a wreck and it was painful and embarrassing to see. "Oh my God." she whispered to herself. "How am I going to hide this; this time."

She closed the visor mirror and closed her eyes. *"While all the time that I was loving you, you were busy loving yourself...."* *"I should have left your ass a long time ago...."*

The lyrics were speaking to her. Why hadn't she left his ass. Why did she allow this? Why did she think that he really loved her? Love shouldn't feel like this. Love shouldn't be this painful. Love shouldn't have her in the middle of nowhere at a gas station beat up with nowhere to go.

A tear fell. Then another one. She dropped her head into her hands and allowed a few more to fall. She didn't want to cry but she couldn't help it. The pain was too overwhelming and the song had taken over her mind.

How could she let herself end up in this kind of situation. Again. She remembered the last time she said it was going to be the last time. That was six months ago and here she is again telling herself that this was going to be the last time.

She wiped the tears with the back of her hand. She picked up the phone. She couldn't just sit there all night and feel sorry for herself. She had to find somewhere to go.

Her phone flashed again. It was him again. She angrily swiped the screen to ignore the call and then she yelled out "You fucking bastard!" She was yelling at the phone but not talking to anyone.

She could have answered it and said it to him but he wasn't worth it. He didn't deserve the energy or the words. He didn't need to know that she was angry and weak and emotional. She wasn't going to give him the satisfaction of even hearing her voice.

She tapped the screen to pull up her contacts list and began to scroll through the list of names. Who could she call. It's two o clock am and most of her friends were sleep. She can't go home because she shared a home with him. Her mom was out of the question. She wasn't ready to face her family with the truth about what she had been going through with him. Especially not looking and feeling the way she did at this very moment.

As she scrolled through the list of contacts in her phone she replayed the scene over and over again in her mind. How could she let this happen again......?

Chapter 2

Briana

This is Mine

Earlier that night.......

She pulled her car into her parking spot in the driveway connected to the garage in front of her house. She had just made it home from work and was running a little late.

She parked the car and got out adjusting the black pencil skirt she was wearing. She grabbed her purse, keys, and lunch bag and locked the car door with the automatic lock on her key ring. Once she heard the chirp and click sound which meant the car was locked and the alarm was on she walked to the front door of the house.

She put her key in the lock and then checked the mailbox. She was glad the mailbox was empty because her hands were full. She unlocked the door and walked into the house. "Bry" she said loudly.

Bryan Paul Tate her boyfriend of six years walked out of the kitchen with soapy hands drying his hands on a towel. Bryan is a very handsome six-foot-tall cross between Tyson Beckford and Bryce Wilson as far as looks.

He has almond skin, slim brown eyes and black naturally wavy hair that he keeps faded with a tight lining.

Standing in the kitchen doorway he said "What took you so long Bri?" with an irritated tone.

"Bri" short for Briana is what he called her.

"Sorry I am late; I was in traffic babe" Briana responded with a sweet soft voice.

"Bri it doesn't take that long for you to get here even in traffic ma." Bryan said. His tenor voice and east coast accent echoing through the house.

Briana closed the door and locked it; then she set her purse on the lazy boy chair. *Here we go.* she thought.

She said. "Hi to you too baby how was your day?"

Bryan stood there and stared at her. He squinted his eyes and asked "Where you been Bri?"

Briana sucked her teeth. "I already told you I was in traffic. I am only 20 minutes later than I usually get home Bry."

"You better not be lying to me Bri" He said pointing his finger at her.

Briana sighed. She hated when he did that. She hated when

he questioned everything she did. Bryan knows where she is at all times of the day, so she feels that some of his questions are ridiculous. *Why does your make-up look smudged? Are you sure you have been at work? Why are your pants so tight? Who are you trying to impress?*

His constant questioning and accusations would really work her nerves, and lately she had been growing very tired of it.

They have been together for six years, and they have been engaged for four out of the six years. In the beginning it was good. But after they were engaged it seemed that things started to slowly fall apart. Mostly because of Bryan's poor choices and actions.

Bryan stood there staring at her looking for a reason to be mad. She masked her irritation with a smile. Her eyes stared back at him with much love in them. After six years and a lot of drama he was still sexy to her.

His full lips. His shoulder and upper arm sleeve tattoo. The diamond earring that he sported in his right ear. The black NY fitted baseball cap he loved to wear. His wheat colored Timberlands. The way he trimmed his mustache and beard into a goatee. How he's in his early thirties but looks only 24 years old. She loves everything about how he looks.

They shared a brief moment of silence. Briana tilted her head to the side and looked at Bryan standing there with his arm muscles bulging out of the white wife beater t-shirt he had tucked into his dark wash polo jeans.

Without losing eye contact she started walking towards him seductively. Her 5 inch black heels clicked with every step against the hard wood floor. She walked through the living room and dining room to the kitchen doorway where he was standing making sure her flat stomach and curves swayed with every step, never loosing eye contact.

Her black pencil skirt was hugging her curvy frame, so she knew she could catch his attention walking like that and hopefully change the subject.

He started eyeballing her creamy caramel skin, light brown eyes, full lips, flat stomach, and curvy waist. The way her d cup breasts fit in her sky blue button up blouse. Bryan would always get turned on by her walk especially in heels. He loved the way Briana could be so sexy in subtle ways.

She walked up to him and wrapped her arms around him; then kissed him softly on the lips leaving nude Mac lip gloss on his lips and said "No baby; I love you." In her cute baby voice.

Her way of flirting. She placed her hands on his muscular chest, and leaned her head back to look him in the eyes.

Briana is 5'5 but her heels make her about 5'10. She still had to look up at him even in her heels. Her 20 inch jet black hair weave ponytail dangled behind her as she stared into his eyes; wanting him to believe her. Wanting him to stop trying to start some mess so they could get on with their night.

That made Bryan weak and he softened his stare. He clutched her ass and cupped it aggressively with one hand starring her right in her eyes as to say *This is mine.* Without saying the words.

His hood swag turned her on sometimes. *Thank God.* She thought to herself knowing he had backed down. She didn't feel like arguing or re explaining herself over and over again until she had a migraine headache.

She would tell him that she got out of a meeting late; which was true, but no matter what she said to him he was going to find some way of turning it into a lie. He kissed her again and released her gently moving her out of the way so he could start getting ready to leave.

As long as he didn't start an argument she was cool because it is the arguments that always lead to more stuff. The argument would get heated and then it would get physical. Usually he would be the one to lose his temper and get physical.

They really didn't argue too much in the beginning. It wasn't until after Briana found out that he was cheating when things took a turn for the worst.

Briana should have left him after she found out about the first girl, or even the first time he put his hands on her. She stayed. Thinking that eventually things would change and things would get better. Believing that he would change, because every time something happened that's what he promised to do, but he was never able to keep that promise.

Briana knows that she hasn't always been an angel but Bryan is for damn sure not a saint. Bryan's insecurities didn't kick in until he started cheating on her. Briana trusted Bryan until she found out he was cheating. After all his lies, cheating, and abuse she had a very brief moment of non-innocence. He found out. Made him even more aggressive, controlling, and insecure.

"Are you ready to go Bri? We are running late." Bryan said.

"Yes. Where are my babies at?" Briana said turning towards

the refrigerator.

"They are in their room." Bryan said then called their names.

"Daaaisia." "Daaalila." Bryan called out. He put the dish towel on the counter and went up the stairs connected to the kitchen to get his things for work.

The second floor level of their house just had one bedroom that they turned into an office slash storage area where they kept all of the things that they couldn't fit in their bedroom. Like Briana's excessive shoe collection and all of Bryan's books and reading materials. The office has a desk with a computer, file cabinet, copy and print machine, and a bookshelf.

The main level of the house is where Briana and Bryan's bedroom is located. The main level is where the kitchen is located complete with a sliding door that leads to the patio and the backyard. The dining room, living room, and one of the bathrooms are also on the main level. The lower level of the house is a finished basement and has a bedroom, bathroom, and laundry room. The lower level was Daisia and Dalila's area of the house.

Daisia and Dalila are Bryan's 12-year-old twin daughters from a previous relationship. Bryan and Briana have been raising them since they were 6 years old. He and the mother made arrangements so he could have them full time.

The twins were a handful to Briana when they first arrived, but over the years she has grown to love them like they were her own. Now, she didn't know what she would do without those girls. They were her everything and sometimes she thinks she may have stayed in the relationship with Bryan so long just for them.

Briana removed her shoes and then walked back into the living room with the apple she grabbed from the refrigerator. She sat down on the leather couch to wait for Bryan and the girls. She heard the girls foots steps coming up the stairs from the lower level of their house.

"Hey step mommy!" They said in unison walking into the living room.

Briana admired that twin bond. They spoke together and finished each other sentences. It was cute to Briana.

Excited to see her girls she perked up "Hey my babies!" she said smiling at them. She called them her babies even though they weren't hers and they were barely babies anymore. The twins love it.

Briana looked at them and thought to herself *they are so pretty*. She had thought that about them many times over the years as she watched them grow into beautiful young ladies. She tells them every day how beautiful they are. Sometimes she wished that they were her daughters.

The twins look just like their father. They have their fathers almond skin, brown slanted eyes, dark hair, and full lips. They both stand close to 5'3 and both slim framed with no hips. Their bodies just starting to develop. Both of them starting to get breasts. One of the twins is a little more developed than the other, but they are identical. It is hard for people to figure out which one is which but Briana and Bryan know who is who.

Although the twins are identical, they are very different in a lot of ways. Bryan and Briana noticed over the years that they look the same, but their personalities were completely opposite. That's how they are able to differentiate the two of them besides some of their physical differences.

People always say there is a good twin and a bad twin. Briana and Bryan believed this to be true. Dalila "The good twin." Was like what her name means. "Gentle." She was soft spoken and much quieter than her twin sister. She liked to read and stay to herself most of the time.

Daisia "The bad twin." totally opposite than her sister. She was sassy and way beyond her years. She liked to watch reality shows and talk on the phone. She is always *"In grown folk's business."* Their grandma would say. They both were born with the same voice and looks but they were two different people.

The twins ran to Briana arms outstretched wanting hugs. Without standing up she stretched her arms out to hug them both. They jumped into Briana's arms giggling. They loved Briana beyond words.

Both twins were rocking freshly flat ironed wrap styled natural hair that hung down to their shoulders. Both of them were wearing the latest Jordan sneakers on their feet, skinny jeans, and a hooded designer sweater. Dalila was wearing a black sweater and Daisia was wearing a red one.

"Well don't you girls look pretty." Briana said.

"Daddy got our hair done today." Daisia said.

"Let me see spin around." The twins spun slowly so Briana could check out their hair.

"I love it!" She said and stood up to hug them both.

"Did your daddy take ya'll to Sasha's?"

"Yes." They said in unison.

"Daddy said we are coming to work with ya'll tonight." Dalila said.

Briana walked over towards the door so she could find some comfortable flat shoes to wear.

"Oh yea? Well good cause we are gonna put you two to work and mess that pretty little

hair up." Briana said jokingly.

Daisia put her hand on her side and said. "Uh a no ma'am not this hair." Swinging her head side to side with her eyebrows up imitating her favorite character from one of the reality shows she likes to watch.

"Be quiet little girl." Briana said laughing.

"You watch too much TV now go and put your jackets on you two, we are about to go soon and it's a little chilly outside." she told the twins.

It was nearing winter time in Minnesota so the snow hadn't fell yet, but the temperatures were dropping from summer season. Daytime during the fall/winter transition is sometimes nice enough to not have to wear a sweater or a jacket. At night, fall season can be a little nippy.

"Let's go girls." Bryan called out walking towards the door with his work bag in hand. They all left out of the door and piled into the car.

Chapter 3

Briana

I Can't Do This Anymore

Briana, Daisia, and Dalila sat on top of one of the many tables in the office building watching Bryan work.

Briana and the girls really didn't do much when on Bryan's job but clean a few windows and dust a few corners if he needed them to. For the most part they just hung out. It was fun for the twins because they could talk Briana's ear off and tell her about everything she missed during the week while she was at work.

They would laugh and giggle and have girl talk. Briana enjoyed hearing them talk. It was amazing to her how much they have grown over the years. They were turning into some beautiful young ladies under the careful supervision of their father and her.

Bryan made good money running his own business, and he had a few side hustles going on that kept her and the girls taken care of. He was always running around doing this and doing that. He stayed in a meeting somewhere with someone different all the time.

Bryan was always making business moves. Always making something happen to keep his money flowing. He didn't have a degree. He didn't work in some big cooperate office. He figured out how to make money on his own and he was good at it.

Bryan is business minded. Briana admires that about him. She would sometimes just sit and watch him and get lost in the essence of him. She loved to hear him on the phone handling business with different people; setting up meetings and creating different ways to make his cash flow.

Briana's phone vibrated on the desk beside her. *Damn* she thought. She forgot to put it on silent or leave it in the car. Every time her phone rings no matter who it is Bryan started getting suspicious. She learned over time that if she kept the phone quiet and out of sight he wouldn't have to question. Because of Bryan; her motto is out of sight out of mind.

She knew right now that whether she ignored it or answered it; Bryan would raise his eyebrows.

Briana picked up the phone and swiped the screen. It was a text message from one of her two best friends Mercedes.

Mercedes:

What you doing next weekend?

Briana:

I'll probably be with Bryan and the girls.

Mercedes:

Uuugh do you ever get away from him? Anyways I know you didn't forget about my birthday next weekend bitch and I know you are coming because you never miss my birthday.

Briana:

Whatever yes I do and no I didn't forget I will be there.

Briana set her phone back down on the table and focused her attention back on the girls. Bryan looked back at Briana and noticed her setting her phone down. She looked up at him knowing he was watching. He gave her eye contact with no expression on his face and then turned away. Bryan continue to work moving towards the back rooms of the building. Briana knew that he was irritated but played it cool in front of the girls.

Daisia said. "Bri you missed Real Housewives of Atlanta last night."

Briana started playfully shaking Daisia by the shoulders. "You know your daddy doesn't like you watching that show."

She gave Daisia a serious face and then said in a lower voice "Anyways so what happened?"

All three of them laughed.

"Well see NeNe-"

"Bri." That was Bryan interrupting Dasia in mid-sentence. Calling for Briana to come to the back room where he was.

"Come here for a second I need your help with something." Bryan said.

Briana looked at Dasia and said. "I'll be right back babe and then you can finish telling me ok?"

Daisia nodded her head yes and smiled. Briana dropped down from the table they were sitting on and walked towards the back of the building where Bryan was.

Bryan knew he didn't need help he just wanted to get her away from the girls so he could interrogate her some more about her whereabouts earlier. Especially since she got some suspicious text to her phone just a minute ago.

The text wasn't *really* suspicious, but, in his eyes any text is suspicious because he can't see it. She could swear sometimes it felt like she was in court, or on trial, and in some detective's interrogation room dealing with Bryan.

"Yes Bry." Briana said calmly as she was entering the room he was working in.

Bryan stopped working and looked Briana in the eyes.

"Close the door." Briana closed the door gently.

"Where were you earlier?"

"Are you serious Bry? I was at work and you know that."

"No I don't know that. What took you so long to get home?"

"I already explained that Bryan when I called you."

"You're never late Bri."

"The meeting at work ran over a little."

"I think you are lying."

"Oh my God Bryan I am not lying." Briana said starting to get irritated, but she kept her voice calm. She did not want to escalate the conversation. Briana just wanted him to leave her alone about her being late. She did not feel like going over it again and again which she has to do most times just to make him feel comfortable.

"Who was texting you?"

Briana knew that question was coming.

"Mercedes."

"You know I don't like you talking to that bitch."

Bryan doesn't like Mercedes because she is a little on the wild side.

"Don't disrespect her Bryan."

"I call it how I see it."

Briana shook her head. "I don't want to do this right now Bryan."

She turned to walk out of the door. Bryan grabbed her arm and snatched her back to him with all his strength. Clenching his teeth, he said. "Don't walk away from me when I am talking to you." Bryan's tall muscular frame standing over her. Briana felt pain from him squeezing her arm and began to get nervous.

"I don't want to stand here and listen to you disrespect my friend." She said in a low voice.

Bryan doesn't just have anger problems but he also has control issues. Briana knows this and tries her best to avoid these situations. She didn't know what he was going to do next. His actions had been unpredictable lately. She didn't want to do anything to set him off especially with the girls there.

Most of the time he would not do anything crazy around them protecting his image for his daughters. Bryan didn't want them to see what kind of man he *really* was. He didn't want them to hate him for the rest of their lives. But lately Bryan had been something else.

Briana looked at him with pleading eyes. "Brian let me go." she said in a whisper. Her voice beginning to quiver. Tears starting to fill her eyes.

"Are you going to do this with your daughters on the other side of the door?" Briana said. Her eyes begging him to cool out. He gave her direct eye contact driving the point that he was not playing with her and then pushed her towards the door.

"We'll talk about this later Bri." Bryan said.

Briana didn't look back she just walked out the door adjusting her clothes. Fighting back the tears trying to form in her eyes. Questioning herself why hadn't she left the phone in the car or put it on silent.

She walked straight into the bathroom that was across the hall from the room she and Bryan were in before going back to the front of the building where the girls were. She looked in the mirror and took a deep breath; letting it out slow trying to slow down her heart rate. She whispered to herself in the mirror. "I can't do this anymore."

Briana was tired. Tired of the drama, tired of walking on egg shells around this man, tired of covering up bruises, tired of being nervous, tired of him controlling everything in her life. Not being able to do or say the things she wanted without worrying about what he would do. Briana
was over it.

She adjusted her clothing and grabbed a tissue to dab the tears that threatened to fall. Taking another deep breath, she walked out of the bathroom towards the front of the building where the twins were.

"What y'all doing out here?" She asked trying to sound upbeat.

"Nothing. "They responded in unison.

"Are you ok step mommy?" Dasia said looking towards the back of the building where their daddy was.

"Yes baby I am. Ok so finish telling me about the show." Briana said changing the subject.

Briana sat and listened to her give Briana a play by play on who talked about who, and who got into an argument, and why this person was mad at that person. All three of them laughed and talked until it was time to go.

Chapter 4

Briana

I am done

It was getting late and they were almost done with the last place they had to go to for the night. They all split up so they could get it done fast. They were all tired and ready to go home.

That is probably why Briana decided to keep her phone on her instead of leaving it in the car like she usually does. After the little situation earlier in the night, Briana knew that leaving the phone in the car would have been the best decision. Briana chose to go against her first mind and brought it with her anyways.

The twins were on the other side of the building doing some dusting and Briana was cleaning some tables. Bryan was vacuuming the carpets.

Briana stopped to text her other best friend Imani whom had text her while she was driving earlier. Imani's text message to her while she was driving had been one of the reasons she decided to bring her phone in with her. Briana wanted to talk to her girl, so she put the phone on silent. She figured Bryan was busy and wouldn't notice her text messaging Imani back. Imani was just confirming if Briana would be at Mercedes birthday get together the next weekend.

Bryan came around the corner and turned off the vacuum.

"Give me your phone."

Briana turned to Bryan and looked at him. She thought he was too busy to notice her texting Imani. He had been around the corner. Briana figured she had enough time to text her friend back without him noticing. She should have known better than that. Bryan watches her every move like a hawk.

"Why?"

Briana was getting annoyed with his shit. She was tired and at this point she felt like he could do whatever it was that he was going to do but she wasn't going to back down no more. She was done with being soft and trying to calm him and make him believe and understand that her love for him was deep. Briana was tired of hiding her phone. She was tired of adjusting her clothes. She was tired of looking at the floor whenever other men were around.

"Because I wanna know who you are texting ma."

"So just ask me."

"I want to see for myself."

"Why can't you just trust me Bry?"

Briana's voice was starting to sound agitated. Briana felt that if anybody should be doing the questioning it should have been her questioning Bryan. Somehow Bryan always turned it on her, even though, Bryan was the one who was unfaithful in their relationship.

"I am getting sick and tired of this Bry, I wasn't talking to anybody but Imani and Mercedes."

"I want to see for myself Bri."

"No Bry I am not a little girl and you are not my daddy your girls are on the other side of this building. I am a grown woman and I am telling you that I am not doing anything behind your back. I love you and only you but you have got to stop accusing me and trust me. I have never cheated on you."

Briana's voice was a little louder and more stern. She was giving him direct eye contact. She wanted him to understand that she was serious. Briana knew she could just give him the phone and end this, but Bryan would find something else to trip about another day.

"You were wit my boy."

"Wow so you are bringing up old stuff now?"

"That's why I don't trust you."

"Do I bring up the shit you did? I never slept with him and you know that. He

was my friend just like he was yours."

"You shouldn't have been with him at all."

"You're right and you shouldn't have been with the women you were with either."

"Give me your phone Bri."

"No."

Bryan's eyes darkened. He was losing control of the situation and he didn't like it.

"I'm not gonna ask you again Briana. First you were late and now you runnin around hea being sneaky wit ya phone."

"I am not being sneaky. I am talking to *my friends* and *I* can do that."

Briana started emphasizing her words.

"About what?"

"Does it matter?!"

"It does! And if they are asking you to go out; you're not going out with those bitches."

"Yes I am and don't disrespect them, they did nothing to you."

"No the fuck you're not! That bitch Mercedes is a hoe and you're not going end of story, now give me your phone."

"Whatever Bryan, just because Mercedes is a stripper doesn't make her a hoe. What she does is her business I can handle myself. Those are *my friends* and *I am going* if *I* want to."

"Phone Bri."

"No."

"What the fuck did I say?" Bryan said with authority.

Briana sighed and sucked her teeth. She shifted her weight from her right leg to her left. Briana crossed her arms in front of her breast. She was heated. She could feel her body burning up inside.

Her nostrils flared as she looked at this man that she loved and adored. The man that she built a life with. The man she was helping to raise his kids. The man that she once looked up to. The man that right now she couldn't stand. Briana wasn't having it. She wasn't going to let him talk to her like that anymore.

"I am getting so tired of this shit with you Bryan." Her eyes filling up with tears.

"What the fuck *did I* say?" Bryan said.

"Give me *your* phone Bry?" Briana responded.

"We are not talking about me right now."

"But we need to be. All these bitches you have messed around on me with and you have the nerve to be asking me for my phone?"

"Phone Bri."

Briana took a deep breath and pushed it out of her nose.

Briana started to hand him the phone but changed her mind. She didn't feel like proving herself again like always. These days she always gave in because she didn't want to fight him. There was a time when she was more argumentative, but after a few altercations she started to back down.

She thought about when he wasn't like this. When he wasn't this person standing in front of her right now. When he was sweet, charming, caring and thoughtful. Before he became this monster. She missed those days.

Then she got a flash back of the last time they were in this kind of situation. Having a heated conversation in a work place. She ended up on the bathroom floor crying after he smacked her and pushed her in there by her neck threatening her to move or try to come out so he could fuck her up. The girls weren't there that time. She remembered thinking she may not have come out of that bathroom alive.

Bryan stepped closer to her. "Bri what did I say?"

"You know what Bryan at this point I don't care."

"What did you just say?"

"I'm done Bryan. I can't do this anymore."

She turned and started walking towards the exit; arms still folded and face frowned.

"Done with who Briana?" He said in a serious but calm tone.

"Done with me? Huh?" Bryan asked.

Before she could get a few steps away from him he stormed towards her and yanked her backwards by her ponytail.

"You think you gonna leave me!" He spat at her.

Briana lost her balance and fell to the floor landing on her back. Her cell phone flew out of her hand and slid across the office carpet.

She scrambled backwards trying to get back on her feet.

"Bryan Stop!" she yelled as he slammed the palms of his hands onto her chest to grip her shirt lifting her up off the floor slamming her into the wall.

"You can't leave me! You're mine you hear me! You belong to me! Do you know who the fuck made you huh?! I made you Bri!" Bryan said with his teeth clinched together and only his lips moving.

His face was close to hers. His forehead touching her forehead. Looking her right in the eyes. He grabbed her by her face squeezing her cheeks together.

"Look at me! You're mine Bri!"

Briana started putting up a fight swinging her arms and

kicking her legs. She was just making him madder. She was kicking and punching and squirming. As they were tussling, she hit him a couple of times not fazing him at all. Bryan reached back and smacked her so hard her face flew to one side and her eyes started welling up with tears.

Briana who was swinging and kicking; got a good kick in. Right between his legs. When he felt the pain he let go of her grabbing his man hood. "Ahhh bitch" he said doubling over in pain.

Briana scrambled to quickly grabbed her cell phone and ran out the door. Shaking so bad she could barely get the key into the ignition of her car to start it. She started the car thanking God she had the car key tucked in her bra and he didn't rip it off. She was so glad that her purse was already in the trunk of the car. She put the car in reverse; sped backwards to back out; then put the car into drive and sped off towards the highway.

Chapter 5

Malik

Love is Blind

Still sitting at the gas station. Briana wiped her eyes on her ripped shirt. "Look at this shit" she said fingering the torn sleeve. It was her favorite button up three quarter sleeve shirt she bought from one of those fancy boutique style stores she loved to shop in. She always wore it with the high waist skirt she was wearing.

She had to find somewhere to go. She thought about calling one of her best friends Imani, but Imani would freak out and want to call the police and she didn't want to do that. She definitely was not going to call her other best friend Mercedes because Mercedes would want to grab her gun and pop him or call one of her dudes to pop him and she wasn't trying to have her or her friend in jail.

Briana didn't want them to know. She really didn't want anyone to know. She just wanted to go somewhere and hide for a while. Where no one could find her or see her, so she could forget about it and move on with her life; without having to answer questions or deal with the police or go to court. She just wanted to be left alone to deal with it by herself.

She continued to scroll through her list of contacts until she got to Malik's name. Malik is her coworker and friend that she met almost a year ago. She confided in him over lunch one day and they have been friends ever since. He promised her he would keep her secret that she was in an abusive relationship.

They became really good friends over the time they have been working together. Malik had become her shoulder to cry on and she knew she could trust him. Malik had never tried to come on to Briana in any way. He had always been a listening ear.

She would be embarrassed to let him see her looking the way she does, but she needed somewhere to go. She tapped Malik's name and the phone dialed his number.

"Please answer." she whispered.

She had been sitting at the gas station for about 20 min. She was exhausted and wanted to rest.

"Hello." Malik answered his voice low and groggy.

"Malik." Briana said in a soft voice trying not to break down.

"What's wrong B?"

"Um. Do you have company over?"

"Why?"

"Uh…." Briana couldn't get the words out

"It's him again isn't it? Where are you B?"

"Yes." she said wiping a tear from her eye. Her voice was

starting to quiver.

She said. "I am at a gas station; I think I am in Saint Louis park. Can I come over? I have nowhere to go."

Malik grunted as he lifted up in the bed and placed his feet on the floor. He sighed placing his head in his hands sitting on the edge of the bed. He looked to the right at the clock on his nightstand. The red numbers read 3:00am. He knew it was serious because she never called this late, and she would never call this late and ask to come over.

"Come on B." He said his voice deep like Barry White.

Briana said. "Ok could you text me your address? I will have to use my phone navigation to get there."

"Alright." Malik said.

Briana disconnected the phone call. Malik's text message came in with his address a few seconds later. Briana put the address in the maps navigation app on her phone, then, she put on her seat belt, put the car in reverse, and began driving back towards the highway heading to Malik's house.

Malik lived in Brooklyn Park and her navigation said it would take about twenty-five minutes to get there. She turned the radio back up, then turned on her blinker to make a left turn at the stop light. Briana then merged onto highway 100 to begin her drive to Malik's.

Malik was tired and hated being woken up but he knew he had to be there for his friend. Now that he was up, he felt alarmed and concerned because he didn't know what was going on. Based on the things that Briana had already shared with him about

Bryan he knew this couldn't be anything good.

He stood up and went to his closet to put a robe on over his flannel pajama pants and his black wife beater t-shirt. He clicked on the lamp in his room so he could locate his house slippers. He found them and put them on his feet and headed to the bathroom to mouthwash really quick before she got there.

He placed his shoulder length locks in a bun and ran a hot wash rag over his face. He looked at himself in the mirror. He was handsome with smooth chocolate skin, dark eyes, and juicy thick lips. He rubbed his hand over his neatly lined and trimmed full beard. He placed the rag on the sink, turned to leave the bathroom, and clicked the light switch off.

Malik decided to go light some of his candles and incense to bring some positive energy into the apartment. He also pulled out a bundle of sage figuring he would need it to clear out the negative energy she was probably going to bring with her. He clicked on the lamp in the living room and sat down on his plushy brown couch to wait for her to arrive.

Almost thirty minutes later Briana buzzed the door to get into the building. He pressed the button in the apt that unlocks the secured doors to let her in the building.

Malik heard a soft knock at the door. He got up from the couch and opened the door to see a bruised Briana.

He whispered "Damn Briana."

Briana collapsed into his arms and started crying uncontrollably. He held her lightly pulling her into the apartment so he could close the door and lock it.

He stood there and held Briana tight and let her cry into his chest. Her body shook as she sobbed. She couldn't control the tears. It was like years of built up hurt, pain, and frustration was all coming out. She cried for a few minutes and he stood there and let her; allowing her to get it all out.

Malik stood there with tears welling up in his eyes. Hurt by what he saw. In disbelief that a man could do this to a woman. He felt for his friend. He squeezed her a little tighter wanting her to know she was safe with him.

She lifted her head to wipe her eyes and said "Sorry Malik."

"Sorry for what?"

"Sorry to bother you."

"You are not bothering me."

He put his hands on her shoulders and pushed her away from his chest "Look at you." Malik said with sadness in his eyes.

"Why do you let him do this to you?" Malik pulled Briana back to him. He wrapped his arm around her shoulder and walked her to the couch.

Malik sat Briana down on the couch, then went to the kitchen. He grabbed a Ziploc bag and filled it with ice. Then he got some paper towel, peroxide, and some gauze. He sat down next to her.

"So what happened?" Malik asked.

Briana began to tell him what happened. Malik gave her the ice bag to hold up to her face over the swollen bruise. He dabbed a little peroxide on the paper towel and he pat it on her chest scratches lightly while listening to her story. He placed the gauze over the scratches and used tape to create a bandage.

He continued to listen as he went back to the kitchen to make another ice bag. He came back to the couch and placed it on her lip.

When Briana finished talking he said. "Are you going to go back to him this time?"

She hesitated then she said. "No."

"Are you sure?"

"Yes."

"Do you want to call the police?"

"No."

"Why?"

"Because the last time I felt like they were laughing at me."

"Why do you say that?"

"They were looking at me like I was stupid. One of the cops had the nerve to say *you know the next time might be the last time* with a smirk on his face. Like he was amused to see a battered black woman."

"You know he was telling the truth right?"

"Well I didn't like the way he said it."

"Sometimes the message isn't always delivered the way you want it to be."

Briana fell silent. Malik left it alone. He didn't want to push too hard. He stood up to go to the kitchen to make them some green tea.

Briana said. "I love him." She had tears in her eyes again.

Malik looked at her and said. "I know that, but when are

you going to realize that sometimes love is blind?"

Briana said. "You're right."

They sat up for another hour. They drank tea. They talked. Briana cried some more. He burned sage. He held her. He wiped her tears. He put on soft jazz. He rubbed her back until she fell asleep.

Then he placed a fluffy blanket over her and one of the plushy pillows from the couch under her head and clicked off the lamp in the living room. After he made sure Briana was comfortable, Malik went to his bedroom clicked off the lamp in his bedroom and laid down to go to sleep. He looked at the clock on his nightstand before closing his eyes it was 5 am.

Chapter 6

Jade

You're Gonna Be My Wife

The same night…….

Jade was asleep in her comfortable California King size bed when her cell phone started ringing. She knew the ring tone but didn't want to be bothered, so she just ignored it acting like she didn't hear it so he would stop calling.

The calls were coming in back to back for 2 min so she sat up groaning and sucking her teeth. She didn't want to talk to Bryan because a few days before they had gotten into an argument about a picture she saw in his phone. When she questioned him about it he got an attitude and stormed out of the door slamming it behind him.

Jade knew when he left she wouldn't hear from him for a couple of days and she was glad. She was still pissed that he had another chicks picture in his phone and what he told her wasn't making any sense.

Jade picked up the phone with an attitude and answered it

"What Bryan?"

"The fuck you mean what? I know you hear me calling you!"
He yelled into the phone.

"I was sleep Bryan its 2 am." She said with a lot of attitude.

"I don't give a fuck what time it is. You answer when I call."

"Yea whateva nigga."

"Yea whateva? Ok. Open the door." Bryan said.

"Use ya key."

"I don't have it on me."

Jade rolled her eyes and sucked her teeth. With the phone
still to her ear she slid out of the bed and tip toed through the condo
to the door. She swung the door open wearing a cami and boy shorts
pajama set.

The turquoise color of the set bounced off of her brown
skin. She just dyed her shoulder length hair blonde and was rocking
a deep side part like most of the reality television stars were doing.

The semi chilly air from the hallway of her building made
her nipples hardened. She wasn't wearing a bra or panties under the
set and that's the way Bryan liked it. He loved the way her firm round
butt hung out of the bottom of the shorts and jiggled when she
walked. His eyes went straight to her nipples and then to her eyes.

"What da fuck did I tell you about answering the door
dressed in shit like that Jersey?"

Bryan called her Jersey because she was from New Jersey
and had just moved to Minnesota a year and a half ago when he met
her. Since her name started with J and she was from Jersey he made
that her special nick name. Plus, it was a name he could save in his

phone that Briana would never detect.

Bryan was attracted to Jade's looks but mostly attracted to her sassy attitude and her New Jersey accent. She reminded him of home back east where he was from.

Jade crossed her arms in front of her; then she turned around and started walking away from the door towards the bedroom. Her booty bounced with every step. Bryan stepped in the condo and closed the door locking it behind him.

"I can wear whateva I want you ain't my daddy." Jade said while walking towards the bedroom.

Bryan walked up on her. "I ain't ya daddy huh? Come mere."

Bryan grabbed her arm and pulled her turning her to face him. He put his lips to hers "What you say ma? You think you got a little attitude?"

Bryan's lips were rubbing against hers with every word. Jade gave him eye contact but didn't speak a word. Jade knew what she was doing and it excited her, but she couldn't show it.

He began kissing her aggressively pushing her towards the bedroom. He cupped both of his hands under her perfectly round butt and lifted her off of the floor. She wrapped her legs around him giving the same aggressive body language he was giving her.

Bryan was giving Jade what she wanted. Jade was mad at Bryan, but the truth was she missed him and her body was craving his touch. She needed to feel his heat, his passion, and his aggression. She wanted him and this make up sex was going to be better than real sex. Jade feels that make up sex is always hotter, more intense, and more passionate.

They made it to the bed; she unwrapped her legs and slid down his body. He laid her on the bed, then he hurriedly unbuckled his belt and allowed his jeans to drop around his ankles resting on top of his timberland boots. He snatched her boy shorts to one side and entered her.

He began pumping aggressively in and out of her. Giving her body what it was craving. Jade didn't flinch she accepted him and rode with every pump giving it back to him the same way he was giving it to her. She opened her legs wider and grabbed his butt pushing him deeper into her.

No moaning could be heard just heavy breathing between them as their bodies fought against each other. They looked each other in the eyes the whole time. Her body talked to him letting him know that she liked it. Bryan knew what she wanted and planned to give it to her.

He pulled out of her. Bryan snatched her boy shorts down her legs and off from her feet. He pulled her feet towards him to pull Jade to the edge of the bed. He then, flipped her onto her stomach.

He entered her again grabbing her hair into a tight grip. Not enough to pull it out but enough to control the motion of her head. Pumping harder and more aggressive he said. "Who ain't ya daddy?"

Out of control now; Jade started gripping the sheets feeling like she was going to scream. She didn't want the neighbors to hear her so she bit into the pillow that was close to her head.

He pulled her hair a little and said "Who's ya daddy?" Pumping a little harder than before.

Jade couldn't take it; she moaned quietly and said. "You."

"What's my name?" Bryan asked louder than before. He smacked her backside making it jiggle.

Jade moaned and then she whispered. "Bryan."

"What's my name!?" he said louder pulling her hair.

"Bryan!" She yelled as her orgasm got the best of her.

She said his name 3 more times. "Bryan, Bryan, Bryan!" In unison with 3 of his strokes. "Ahhh" Jade screamed into the pillow. Feeling the "O" riding the "O" loving the "O."

Her body tensed and then relaxed. Bryan felt her walls tightened and her juices burst onto his manhood. He felt himself about to cum.

"Uuuuuh" He groaned then he pulled out and released his jizzim all over her lower back and butt.

Bryan stepped back breathing hard staring at her laying on the bed breathing hard. Jade's beautiful brown skin glistening with sweat under the moonlight peering through the bedroom window. Jade's body shape was tight and athletic. She had six pack abs, toned legs, toned arms, and the booty of a stripper.

Bryan slid out of his boots, jeans and boxers. He went to the bathroom and put some soap on a washcloth and came back into the room to clean Jade off. Then he went back to the bathroom to clean himself off. Making sure he cleaned himself off really good knowing that Jade would probably give him some head in the morning to wake him up.

Jade took off the top piece of her pajama set. She readjusted the top mattress of her bed that was sort of hanging off of the box spring. She fixed the fitted sheet that was now in the middle of the bed because of her pulling them. After fixing the fitted sheet she made sure the top sheet and blanket were on straight and then climbed underneath.

Bryan walked back into the room and removed his wife beater t-shirt and got into the bed next to Jade. They cuddled in the dark naked. Something they always did after sex. He kissed her on the forehead. She kissed him on the shoulder. He rubbed the tattoo of his name she had on her lower back. She kissed him on the lips.

"You know you're gonna to be my wife ma." he whispered to her drifting off to sleep.

She stared at him in the dark. Admiring his clear skin, his dark hair, and his muscular build. Thinking about how much she loved him. Reminiscing about how they met and how he has been her world ever since.

It had been a year and a half since they met and she had given herself to him wholeheartedly. He had been nothing but good to her. He took care of her, he did anything she asked. He never disrespected her no matter what and she loved that.

She never once gave thought to the fact she had never been to his house. She never pondered on the reason why she had never met his twin daughters. She simply trusted what he told her.

He told her that his mom was living with him so he could take care of her because she was sick. He told her he never invited anyone to his house out of respect for his mom. He told her that his twins stayed busy in after school activities, and extracurricular activities which made them unavailable all the time.

When Jade got into a tight situation with where she was staying, Bryan bought the condo for her; filling it up with all her hearts desires. When he would have a night off from taking care of his mama he would stay the night with Jade or the weekend depending on his mother's needs according to him. He promised her that once they got married he would introduce her to the whole family and she believed him.

But lately something was pulling at her. Something just wasn't right. Jade kept trying to ignore it. Kept trying to push it away and out of her head but it just kept coming back. That something was pulling at her, haunting her, and nauseating her.

Some call it a gut feeling; others call it women's intuition. And after seeing that picture in the phone of that girl he claimed was his cousin, she realized that it matched the picture of the girl her best friend text to her. She knew she wasn't tripping.

Jade waited until Bryan started snoring. She gently and quietly slid out of bed and tip toed to the side of the bed where he left his jeans. She gently pulled his cell phone out the pocket. Without making a noise she crept into the bathroom and shut the door. Bryan was sound asleep.

Chapter 7

Jade

I Told You I Got You Ma

Bryan and Jade met at the local gym. Jade had just moved into town and didn't really know anybody accept her brother and his girlfriend Lisa. Jade lived with them in a house that was just a few blocks from the gym.

Since she was new in town and hadn't yet gotten established, she thought she would busy herself while looking for a job. She loved working out so her brother paid for her to get a membership at the local gym.

Jade hated living with her brother and his girlfriend because she hated his girlfriend Lisa. She always seemed to have some smart shit to say, and she was always picking an argument with Jade's brother. Jade didn't understand why her brother liked that girl but it was none of her business.

It was Jade's brother's idea for her to move to a new city and state so she could get a fresh start. She was ready to get away from home. She wished her brother would have warned her that Lisa was a crazy psycho bitch, and she wasn't going to like her. None the less she was glad that he told her to come because if he hadn't, she probably never would have left home.

She started seeing Bryan at the gym about 2 weeks into going. *He is fine.* She thought to herself the first time she saw him. She secretly watched him working out while she was working out. Checking him out without looking too obvious. Well at least she thought she wasn't being obvious.

She made note as to what time he came to the gym every day and made sure she was there at that time working out in the sexiest workout outfits she had in her drawer. When she wasn't at a treadmill facing him watching him she would be looking at him through the gym mirrors.

They bumped into each other leaving the locker room one day. Well, Bryan *really* waited for her to come out of the locker room. He noticed her watching him and figured that he would ask her for her phone number.

"What's up ma?" Bryan said.

"What's up." Jade said. She turned to face him.

"I'm Bryan what's ya name?"

"Why?" Jade asked with a sassy attitude.

"I see you watching me ma just figured I'd introduce myself."

Jade laughed "Oh you see me watchin you? Get outta hea"

Jade started walking away. Knowing he was right but she had to play hard to get.

"Oh so you gonna just walk away? I can't get ya name or ya numba?"

Jade turned around and looked at him over her shoulder.

"We'll see." She said with a flirtatious smile.

"We'll see what?"

"If we see each other again."

"Yea aight" Bryan said with a smile.

Jade began walking up the stairs towards the door to leave.

"A'yo where you from?" He called after her.

"Jersey." Jade replied as she left out the door.

****

Jade purposely did not go to the gym at her usual time for a couple of weeks to avoid him. Since he noticed her watching him, she decided it would be best to save herself from looking too desperate.

She finally showed up one day and there he was as usual over by the weights. She walked in wearing her black and pink sports bra and matching black and pink workout shorts. Purposely bouncing her booty with every step as she walked towards the treadmills. Her walk did not only catch his attention, but it caught the attention of every man in the gym and a few lesbians.

After her work out she walked to the locker room knowing he would follow. She took her time taking a shower and changing clothes. She walked out of the locker room and there he was.

"Jersey" Bryan said.

"That's not my name."

"Well you didn't tell me ya name ma so I gave you one."

Jade smiled.

"My name is Jade."

"Jade from Jersey huh? Pretty name ma. My name is Bryan and I am from Brooklyn."

She said. "Bryan from Brooklyn huh?" They laughed.

"Nice to meet you." Jade said.

"Likewise, Likewise shorty. Yo I would love to take you out sometime, here's my numba. Call when you're ready."

Jade took the piece of paper and looked at it "Bryan spelled with a Y?"

"Yea you gotta ask my moms about that."

Bryan laughed and Jade giggled.

"Well I gotta break out yo so you got the numba ma. Peace."

Jade instantly loved his confidence and wanted him to be hers. Bryan being from the east was also extremely attractive to Jade. She had already made up her mind that they were going to be together. She just had to play her cards right. She couldn't come off too desperate or too needy so she decided to lay low again and wait awhile before hitting him up.

Jade finally called Bryan after about a week. It drove her crazy every day that she waited because she wanted to talk to him so bad. She couldn't wait to see him again, so when day seven finally came around Jade was on pins and needles.

She wondered what his conversation was going to be like. He already seemed really confident and smooth which made Jade not want to come off too eager to see him or speak to him. She dialed his number with butterflies in her stomach.

"Hello" Bryan answered.

"Hi um Bryan?" Jade said nervously.

"What took you so long to call me ma?"

"Huh? How do you know who this is?"

"Because I know Jersey"

She smiled.

"That put a smile on ya face huh?"

Jade sucked her teeth. "Nah."

"Aight ma so what took you so long to call?"

"I've just been busy is all."

She was lying. She really didn't have a life but she didn't want him to know that.

"Yea aight I see you like playing hard to get. That's cool." He chuckled.

He invited her out to dinner and she accepted the invite. A few hours later he picked her up in his black Range Rover. He looked so good to her dressed in his best casual black suit jacket, button up shirt with no tie, top two buttons opened, jeans, and casual black shoes.

She wore an all-black form fitted mini dress, black leather thigh high stiletto boots and silver hoop earrings to match the silver bangle bracelets on her arm. Her fingernails were polished silver. She did a fierce smoky eye make-up job with hot pink lipstick. She wore her jet black hair flat ironed straight and combed straight back with no bangs.

Jade was impressed with Bryan, and Bryan was impressed with Jade. They had never seen each other outside of the gym so the attraction level went up 10 notches for the both of them when they saw each other.

Bryan loved her body shape and her almond shaped dark brown eyes. He made up his mind at that moment that she was going to be his, and was willing to do whatever it took to have her.

Bryan didn't know that Jade already knew from day one that she wanted to be his. She had already imagined their life together. She had already imagined them walking down the aisle and spending their honeymoon on a beautiful island. She already pictured them taking trips together; spending endless nights and days together. Happy and in love without a care in the world. She already day dreamed about having a house, a kid, and a puppy with him. And even if the house, the kid, and the puppy didn't happen, she would be happy with just her and him forever.

Bryan took Jade to a fancy restaurant in the downtown Minneapolis area. He was a gentleman the entire time. He opened doors, held her hand, and pulled out chairs. He ordered expensive wine. He allowed her to order anything off of the menu no matter the price. He ordered for them making sure he ordered what she wanted first.

He gave her his full attention including eye contact. He complimented her. He didn't talk too much. He asked her questions about her. He listened completely focusing on her and what she had to say.

When dinner was over Bryan drove her home. He didn't

make any sexual advances and didn't ask Jade for a kiss. He told Jade that he had a great time and hoped to see her again soon. Bryan walked Jade to her door and gave her a warm hug telling her that he would call her later. Bryan waited until Jade was safely in the house before driving away.

Jade felt so special. Bryan had her riding on a natural high. She was on cloud nine smiling from ear to ear. Jade was feeling Bryan. From that day forward Jade was all about Bryan and in her mind nothing was going to change that.

Jade and Bryan had spent so much time together. In Jade's eyes there was no way he was spending his time with anyone else. He called her every day. Sometimes several times during the day. Just to tell her he was thinking about her or to tell her how much he was missing her and couldn't wait to see her. He took her out all the time. He showered her with expensive gifts like the latest fashions, shoes, purses, and jewelry.

Bryan took her out constantly. He took her to concerts, movies, dinners, and plays. Bryan spoiled Jade and she loved it. The whole time she never had a clue that Bryan was in a committed relationship with another woman.

Jade figured Lisa was jealous because she kept giving Jade the stink eye and rolling her eyes whenever Jade came back from hanging out with Bryan. Jade felt like it wasn't her fault that Bryan treated Jade better than Jade's brother treated Lisa. It wasn't her fault that Bryan catered to her and gave her more in three months than Jade's brother had ever did for his Lisa in the three years that they were together.

Jade heard Lisa mumble under her breath when Jade was leaving with Bryan one day.

"Hoe fucking for purses and shoes." Lisa said under her breath.

Lisa was wrong because Jade and Bryan hadn't had sex yet. Jade was walking towards the front door. She stopped in her tracks and said. "What?"

Lisa just kept walking towards the bedroom.

"No that bitch didn't." Jade said to herself scratching the back of her head. She rolled her eyes and walked out of the door making a mental note to talk to her brother about it some other time.

"Imma have ta snatch that bitch." Jade said to Bryan. They were in the car on the way to a concert. Bryan let Jade drive that night and she was pushing his whip like it was hers. Bryan liked the way Jade looked driving his Range. She looked so regal.

Bryan chuckled. "Calm down ma."

"Nah she really doesn't know, she fuckin wit tha wrong one." Jade said eyebrows frowned.

"Every time she around me she got something to say, it's like she jealous or something."

"Um hum." Bryan said.

"I might just have ta go back home to Jersey cause I can't keep dealin wit that bitch."

Jade said anger all over her face.

Bryan looked over at Jade and said. "Naw mama don't talk like that, you ain't going nowhere trust me." He rubbed her face making her smile. She parked the truck and they went into the concert.

That was a year and a half ago. The first night they made love. Three months before she had to "Beat that bitch's ass for talkin shit." In Jade's words.

Jade and Lisa exchanged fists while Jade's brother desperately tried to break them up. Jade gave her the beat down she deserved, then, packed her stuff and checked into a hotel. A week later Bryan gave her a key to the condo.

"I told you I got you ma." Bryan said smiling with the key dangling off his finger. He was watching Jade walk through the empty space in admiration.

Jade, overwhelmed with joy made love to him in the middle of the floor in the empty condo. That was two months before Jade found out she was pregnant. Only to have Bryan make her have an abortion. Bryan claiming it wasn't time.

"It's just not the time yet ma, I got the twins." Bryan said while Jade held back tears. She was devastated but had the abortion to please Bryan.

Bryan had given Jade a life away from home. She didn't have to work. She didn't have to worry about anything because he always made sure she was taken care of. Bryan was all Jade had in the city away from her home.

She didn't talk to her brother as much after the altercation she had with his girlfriend. She made one friend; a girl who lived in the same building. She was the only person Jade talked to outside of Bryan. Bryan was her world.

Now, Jade was in the bathroom at 4 am trying to answer the

questions brewing inside of her mind. She was determined to find out what she wanted to know.

Chapter 8

Malik

What'cha Gonna Do Now

Sunlight crept through the blinds. Not bright enough to illuminate the apartment, but light enough to indicate it was in between morning and afternoon. A light aroma of incense drifted through the apartment waking Briana from her sleep. She slowly opened her eyes a little but didn't move because her body felt heavy. She felt like she had been hit with a ton of bricks ten times.

Her eyes slowly adjusted to her surroundings reminding her that she wasn't at home. She had almost forgot where she was until she noticed the African statue in the corner of the living room. *Malik's house* she thought to herself wiping sleep from her eyes.

Flash backs of the night before started to flood her brain reminding her of why she was there. She closed her eyes trying to block it out but the thoughts forced themselves in. Tears burned her already dry and swollen eyes from crying before falling asleep while Malik's magical hands went to work on her back and shoulders some hours ago.

Briana used a corner of the blanket she had over her to dab her eyes. She lifted up from the pillow and sat up straight. She looked around the one-bedroom apartment and noticed the incense smoke coming from Malik's bedroom.

She stood up and quietly tiptoed to Malik's room. She peeked her head in about to say good morning. Malik was sitting on a pillow on the floor with his legs crossed, eyes closed and head bowed in deep meditation and prayer. She decided not to bother him and went back to the couch.

She laid down and heard her phone vibrate. She hadn't thought about her phone since she started driving to Malik's house. She grabbed her purse and pulled her phone out. As usual Bryan had called back to back until he got tired, and if that wasn't enough he left text messages and voicemails in between the calls.

He always did that after he hurt her. He always called a million times pleading, begging, and apologizing. He always wanted her to know how sorry he was. How much he loved her. How much she meant the world to him. How much he needed her, and how he never meant to hurt her. She read a few of the messages and then started to erase them.

"Good morning." Malik said walking into the living room. His deep voice startled Briana and she jumped a little.

"Hi um good morning." Briana said setting her phone down on the arm of the chair.

He laughed a little. "Did I scare you?"

Briana smiled. "Yes you did."

"There goes that smile I like to see. Are you hungry?" Malik asked walking towards the kitchen.

"A little." Briana replied.

Malik walked into the kitchen and began preparing breakfast for the both of them.

"How are you feeling?" He asked Briana while whipping the pancake batter.

"I don't know." Briana said adjusting the blanket over her lap.

She leaned her head back on the back of the sofa and watched Malik work on breakfast in the kitchen. Her eyes evaluated his beautiful tattoo free dark chocolate skin, his toned arms and back, and his dread locks that hung past his shoulders.

She then began to look around the apartment. Book shelf, large plants, African masks and statues. African American art covering the walls even a replica of the painting from the TV show Good Times.

Briana closed her eyes and enjoyed the smell of the breakfast cooking as it began to permeate the apartment. She took in the peaceful atmosphere that Malik had created in his apartment; it made her feel at ease and safe.

Malik's place allowed her to put what had happened out of her mind for a brief moment as she relaxed on the plushy brown couch.

"So what are you going to do now?" Malik asked.

Briana didn't know she hadn't thought about that yet.

"I don't know." she replied without opening her eyes. She started to feel down again. She opened her eyes and looked at him.

"I might have to stay with one of my friends." She said.

"What about your family?" He asked while rinsing out a large bowl.

"I don't really want to see my family."

"Why?"

"They gossip and I don't want them all in my business."

Malik nodded his head a couple of times indicating he understood and began cutting a cantaloupe and a watermelon into pieces. He walked into the bedroom to get his phone.

Walking back into the kitchen Malik logged onto a website that plays nonstop commercial free music of your choice. He then used a USB cord to connect the phone to a pair of small speakers sitting on the kitchen counter. The soulful sounds of Eryka Badu filled the apartment.

After some time had gone by, Malik walked over to Briana with a plate of food. Pancakes, sautéed diced potatoes, wheat toast and fresh fruit.

"Thank You." Briana said.

"No problem." Malik said. Then he grabbed his plate and two glasses and carton of orange juice. He sat on the couch next to Briana and led them in prayer to bless the food.

Although the food Malik prepared was incredible, Briana really didn't have an appetite. She picked around in the food only taking a few bites here and there. Her body felt numb and her mind began to clutter with thoughts of what happened, what could have happened, and what she should do now. It made her sick to her stomach.

Malik broke the silence and said. "You can stay here if you want."

"I can't do that; I will figure something out."

"Well the offer is there if you want it."

"Thank You." Briana said sweetly.

They ate. Malik cleared their plates. He cleaned the kitchen. He handed Briana a towel and one of his sweat suits to change into after she took a shower. She went into the bathroom and peeled off her clothes from the night before. She got the water nice and hot and stepped in.

She showered thinking about Bryan and how it used to be. How happy they were before he messed everything up. Before his attitude changed. Before he had become the selfish cheating asshole of a dog he had turned into.

Briana used some of Malik's soap to wash her body with. Then she cried. She cried hard. One of those soulful cries that come from deep down within. That kind of cry that is supposed to cleanse the soul. She slid down into the tub allowing the water from the shower to beat down over her body, face, and wounds. As the water mixed with her tears she considered filling the tub up so she could drown in it. She figured it would be the best way to escape from the pain and mental anguish she was feeling at the moment.

Malik knocked on the bathroom door breaking her thoughts.

"B? are you ok in there?" He asked Briana through the door.

She hesitated; then she replied. "Yes."

Briana wished she was dead and didn't have to answer him.

"Yes…. Yes, I am ok" She responded again.

"Alright." Malik walked away from the door.

She realized she must have been in there a while for Malik to feel the need to come and check on her. She was in her thoughts and in her feelings and had been sitting there hoping the water would wash her pain away.

Briana slid up in the tub and turned off the water. She stepped out of the tub and dried off with the big fluffy black towel he gave her. She used one of his brushes to brush her hair back into the once beautifully constructed ponytail. Without product there wasn't much she could do with it, but brushing it did enough to make it better than what it was.

Jade put some of Malik's toothpaste to brush her teeth with her finger. She put on the oversized sweatshirt and pants. At that moment she decided that she would have to face it. "I am going to call my girls." She said to herself as she exited the bathroom.

Chapter 9

Briana

A Lady is Supposed to Let a Man Approach Her First

Folding jeans to put them back on the shelf. Folding sweaters to place them back onto the table. Straightening shirts and pants that were on hangers making sure they were color coded and placed in order by size. Smallest to largest; dark colors to light colors. Making sure all the dresses were neatly placed on hangers. Dusting all of the sale signs, fixtures, and pictures.

This is what Briana was doing when she met Bryan. She was working down the check list of duties she had to get done before opening the clothing store she worked in.

Briana looked over at her coworker who was counting the money used to open the register; making sure it was all there.

"You cool over there girl?" Briana asked her coworker.

"Yes I am almost done opening the register. How far along are you?" Her coworker asked.

"I am almost done with the checklist." Briana said walking through the store towards the backroom to grab a bottle of Windex, so she could clean the mirrors that were in the store and in the fitting rooms.

"Ok when I get finished I will sweep the floors." Said her coworker.

Briana's coworker Jolene was a Caucasian girl who had hung around her fair share of black people and it showed in the way she carried herself. How she talked, dressed, even the men she chose to date. Let's just say the men she chose to date were a variety of assorted chocolates. She even cooked soul food.

Briana liked working with her because she was cool and always knew how to get the job done. Since Briana had been promoted to shift supervisor she never gave Briana any drama like some of their other coworkers.

Briana looked towards the front entrance of the store. She always looked out there hoping to see him walk past. The store she worked in was in a mall and he would always walk past around the same time every morning. She figured he must be going to work because he was always dressed really nice. He always wore expensive looking slacks and shoes, different colored ties, button up shirts, and sometimes suits.

"Who are you looking for your boo Briana?" Jolene called out across the store while giggling.

"Girl please I don't know what you are talking about." Briana said and went back to her wiping down the fourth mirror with some paper towel.

"Um hum you know who I am talking about girl. The little cutie you always get googly eyed over, you know I see you." Jolene said placing a stack of already counted five dollar bills into the drawer.

"I know but... SO!" Briana started giggling with her.

"Why don't you just talk to him?" Jolene asked.

"Nooooo I can't do that" Briana said shyly.

"Why not?"

"Because a lady is supposed to let a man approach her first."

"Ok you keep believing that and you are going to miss out on some good men."

"Um hum and you keep on hollering at every man you see; you are gonna end up with ten babies and 9 baby's fathers sitting on the set of Maury." Briana laughed loudly.

Jolene smacked her teeth and threw an ink pen across the store at Briana and said. "Shut up!" Laughing loudly with Briana.

Jolene started sweeping the store while Briana picked up the pen, and then slid all the overstock boxes towards the backroom so they could work on stocking the merchandise later.

Her coworker turned on the rest of the lights in the store. It was time to open so Briana and Jolene walked towards the store to open the gate.

He hadn't walked past yet and he usually walks past before they open the gate. *He must not be coming today.* Briana thought to herself and began adjusting the clothes on one of the mannequins that stood in the front windows.

It was springtime so all of the winter sweaters, scarves, and jackets were on sale in the store. The store was now filling up with short sleeve shirts, shorts, and blouses. All of the merchandise colors were changing from winter blues, grays, and blacks into spring yellows, greens, and pinks.

"Excuse me." A baritone voice said from behind Briana. She was so focused on the mannequin she didn't even see him walk in.

She jumped a little "Hi" She looked up and smiled.

"How are you doing ma, my name is Bryan Tate." He extended his hand.

Briana was taken aback by his approach. She never expected him to come in there or even speak to her. Briana stood there dressed in the stores best fashions because she worked there. Shocked that he was standing there, shocked that he was even talking to her. His beautiful almond skin and brown eyes were captivating to her even more now that he was close up.

She slowly extended her hand to shake his hand and said.

"Hi I am Briana; um Briana Taylor."

She had never had a guy introduce himself by first and last name. Bryan doing that immediately set him apart from other guys.

Bryan looked into Briana's light colored eyes and said.

"Nice to meet you Briana Taylor." His eyes looked her up and down taking in her beauty. A young Briana in her early twenties.

Briana's baby face and caramel skin. Her pink lip gloss on her heart shaped lips, and natural looking makeup, her freshly manicured nails, her natural looking hair weave cut into an asymmetrical bob, and her curvy shape. She wasn't fat but she was thick, mostly on the bottom with a flat stomach.

To be in her early twenties she had the body of a woman in her late twenties or early thirties. Briana was extremely sexy to Bryan and that's why he decided to approach Briana after seeing her so many times. Bryan had to meet her. He hoped Briana didn't have a man.

"Yo I am sorry ma I didn't mean to bother you, I have just been wanting to come in here and say something to you for a while."

Briana smiled. "You're not bothering me." She said softly.

A customer walked in the store and began to look around at the clothes. Briana saw Jolene approach the customer to offer assistance without losing focus on them. *Her nosey ass.* Briana thought to herself and giggled.

"What's funny?" Bryan said smiling at her.

Briana looked back at him. "Oh nothing, I am sorry."

Bryan straightened out his jacket. "Oh I thought I had something on my face or a booger or something." He said.

They laughed.

"No I was laughing at my coworker."

"Oh ok ok let me find out."

They laughed again.

"Look ma I know you are busy but I was wondering if we could like exchange numbers so I can take you out sometime? That is if you don't have a man?"

"Um I don't have a man and that would be cool." Briana responded trying not to sound nervous but she was.

Bryan followed Briana through the store to the register so

that she could write down her cell phone number on one of the stores business cards. Briana handed him the business card with her cell phone number written on it. She gave him an empty business card so that he could write down his cell phone number. After Bryan handed her the business card with his number written on it, Briana walked with him back to the front of the store.

"Nice to meet you beautiful I'll be in touch with you soon ma." Bryan said and then walked out of the store.

Briana watched him as he walked away feeling butterflies fluttering around in her stomach.

"Oooo!" She heard her Jolene squeal with excitement.

"What did he say? What did he say girl?!" Jolene was smiling from ear to ear.

Briana turned around to face Jolene smiling too.

"He said he has been watching me for a while and would like to take me on a date!"

"Yaaay!" Jolene said and hugged her.

"Oh my God girl he is sooo fine!" Briana squealed and then looked over and saw the customer at the register ready to check out.

"I'll be right back." Jolene said rolling her eyes but then plastering on a fake smile before making it to the register. Briana laughed under her breath and then continued to work on the mannequin.

He called her later that day. Her heart jumped when she heard her cell phone ringing. She knew it was him because she didn't get a lot of calls. She was nervous but she answered.

"Hello?"

"How you doing ma?"

"I am fine and you?"

"I am well now that I am talking to you."

Briana giggled.

They talked for a couple of hours going over all the basics. They both were single. They both worked at the mall full time. He was dating, but she wasn't. He lived alone and she lived with her family. He was Twenty -Six years old; a Leo, two kids, from New York. She was Twenty- One, Capricorn, no kids, from Minnesota. They talked until they both were too tired to talk.

Bryan yawned. "I guess I should be going to bed so I can work in the morning." Bryan said barely holding his eyes open.

"Yea me too." Briana yawned and wiped a sleepy tear from her eye.

They both knew they needed to hang up, but didn't want to. He told her to hang up, she told him to hang up; then they both decided to hang up together after counting to three.

****

Bryan took Briana on her first real date that weekend. After talking every day for the rest of that week, and waving at each other every time he walked past the store; they were excited to see each other. Briana was beside herself. She had never really been on a date. Guys her age weren't dating. Their idea of a date was meeting at the club, having a few drinks, and then having alcohol induced sex afterwards at someone's house if it wasn't their own.

Briana wasn't sure what she wanted to wear or how to do her hair. She just knew she wanted to look nice, but not easy. She settled on a pretty yellow and white A-line sundress she bought at the clothing store that she works at. She bought a pair of nude colored wedge open toed sandals to wear with the dress. She wore her hair in a bun with a pretty white flower on the side of the bun.

First they had dinner and drinks; then they went to a different place for dessert. After eating they decided to take a walk around one of Minnesota's 10,000 lakes. Bryan took Briana to her favorite lake. One of the more popular lakes on the Southside of Minneapolis in the uptown area.

She was impressed by him. Maybe because she had never dealt with a man like him. Maybe because she had never dealt with a man at all. All of the guys her age still acted like little boys; that was the primary reason why she was single. Guys her age didn't know how to talk to her or treat her. So even if what Bryan was doing was small to some, it was big to her.

Briana liked that he had a full time job. She like that he had goals to do bigger and better
things in the future. She liked that he had a car and his own place. She enjoyed his company and how he held her hand while they walked around the lake. She was pleased with how much of a gentleman he was. He made her feel on top of the world.

Bryan liked how reserved, sweet, and kind hearted Briana was. Bryan liked Briana's soft spoken voice and calm attitude. He like that she worked and didn't like to go out much. He liked that she was a home-body. Briana was the good girl he had been looking for; for a long time. She made him feel comfortable. He also liked her slight silly side that he knew he could fall in love with.

As they approached the car to leave the lake Bryan stopped Briana from walking and pulled her close while gazing into her eyes.

"Your beautiful ma…. I mean that. I am not saying it just to get your panties because I ain't that kind of guy. I really mean it. It's not just ya looks either, it's your energy and your sprit. You're really beautiful ma real talk."

The butterflies fluttered in Briana's stomach again. Right at that moment he was everything she could have asked for in a man. Her eyes stared back at his while they were standing under the moon light.

"Thank you." Briana said softly.

He pulled her face to his and gently kissed her. She kissed him back. He slipped her a little tongue as he kissed her. She accepted his tongue and gave him a little back. Bryan's kiss made Briana feel weak.

"Briana I don't want this night to end yet, I would love for you to come back to my place. No sex. Just to watch a movie or talk. I just want your company. Will that be ok?" Bryan said to her after kissing her.

Briana didn't want the night to end either but she didn't want to say anything afraid that she would seem too easy, so she didn't answer right away.

Briana thought about it briefly and then she said. "Um that would be fine. I am ok with that."

They went to his apartment after leaving the lake. "Make

yourself at home." Bryan said as he turned on the lights in his apartment.

Bryan locked the door. He went to the kitchen to pour them glasses of wine while Briana removed her shoes and sat on the black leather couch. Bryan walked into the living room and set the glasses of wine on the coffee table putting coasters underneath them. He picked up the remote and turned the power on to the TV.

The screen was already set on a movie website. He handed Briana the remote so that she could choose which movie to watch. Briana looked around the place. His house was so clean for a bachelor. Big screen TV, huge book shelf entertainment center combination, leather furniture, glass tables, beautiful area rugs and hand painted vases.

Everything looked so expensive. Everything was neat and organized accept the men's magazines, fitness magazines, and business books that cluttered the coffee table. The books were the only things out of place.

"Sorry about the books ma, I was studying earlier before I came to get you." Bryan said. He sat down next to Briana on the couch.

"Oh that's ok, you have a very nice place." Briana said. She picked up the wine glass to take a sip of the wine.

He actually reads. Briana thought absorbing the atmosphere. She had never met a guy who actually enjoyed reading.

"Thank You." Bryan responded after he finished taking a sip from his wine glass.

Bryan held Briana in his arms while they sipped on wine,

talked, and watched movies. She felt so good in his arms he didn't want to let her go. So he didn't let her go. He held her until they both fell asleep on the couch.

Bryan was on his back with one foot on the floor and the other one on the couch. Briana's head was on his chest with her body cuddled comfortably between his legs. One of his arms was around her body and the other arm was behind his head.

They woke up the next morning that way. Fully clothed. Bryan woke up before her. He watched her sleep for a little while enjoying her angelic beauty. Her breathing was soft. Her skin was glowing underneath the daylight peeking through the windows. He stared at her long natural eyelashes and heart shaped lips. He admired her pretty fingers and toes polished all white to match her dress. Bryan was feeling Briana. He wasn't sure but at that very moment he felt like he was falling in love.

Bryan kissed Briana's forehead over and over again until she woke up. When she moved he said "Wake up sleeping beauty." in a whisper. Briana opened her eyes slowly looking up at Bryan. He kissed her on the lips.

"I wasn't snoring was I?" She said rubbing her eyes.

Bryan laughed. "No beautiful woman."

Briana lifted up placing her feet on the floor and adjusting her dress.

"There is a tooth brush and tooth paste in the bathroom. If you would like to take a shower, there are towels in the bathroom closet." Bryan told her.

"Thanks." Briana said while standing up to walk to the

bathroom.

Briana closed the bathroom door. She turned on the sink faucet so that the sound of the water would drowned out the sound of her urinating. Briana wiped herself and flushed the toilet; praying that he didn't hear her peeing. She then brushed her teeth but passed on the shower. Briana being a shy woman made her uncomfortable being naked in his bathroom. Partially because they just met, mostly because they hadn't had sex yet. She figured she would just wait until she got home.

Briana readjusted her dress. She took a brush out of her purse to brush the edges of her bun back into place. She reapplied her lip gloss and eyeliner. She checked her appearance in the mirror, then she exited the bathroom and walked back into the living room. Briana smiled at Bryan when she walked into the living room.

"Hey beautiful. Wanna do breakfast ma before I take you home?" Bryan asked.

"Sure." Briana said.

****

Six weeks later Bryan was making love to Briana in between his silk sheets. Slow jams playing in the background. Half empty wine glasses on the night stand next to the bed. Large flat screen TV rested on the fired place channel.

He kissed her slowly on the lips. He tongued kissed her love button. He entered her slowly. Bryan gave her long deep strokes while feasting on her brown nipples. He stared into her eyes. Taking it slow. Making sure that she got hers. He watched her and listened to her sounds knowing it was good to Briana.

When Bryan saw her eyes roll into the back of her head and her head tilt back, he felt her body start to shutter. Bryan knew he hit the spot. He knew she was flying high on that "O". Bryan tapped that spot slow until she came back down to earth. When she did he flipped over and put her on top so he could give her another one.

He grinded upwards into her as she rode his motions. He gripped her hips guiding her movement. They stayed in sync with each other rocking that rhythm slowly until she reached that "O" again. She put her hands on his chest, curving her back, head tilting backwards again, mouth open making sounds of pleasure. He felt her tighten and then plunged deep to short stroke that spot until he released his jizzim into the condom they used for protection.

Afterwards they took a shower together. They washed each other's bodies still tongue kissing. Bryan stepped out of the shower to grab another condom. He slipped it on and bent her over and made love to her in the shower. Soap mixing with warm water, mixing with sounds of love making while the bathroom filled up with steam. She let the water run over her naturally wavy hair as she took it and gave it back.

"I love you Bri." Bryan moaned.

"I love you too Bry." Briana moaned back.

She came again and so did he. They rinsed off and got out of the shower. They dried each other off. He put on silk boxers. She put on the silk nightgown he had bought her. They laid down, cuddled, and drifted off to sleep.

Never Going Back

Chapter 10

Briana

Happy and in Love

Bryan and Briana were inseparable. They spent every night together. Briana never went back home where she lived with her family. She would stop by there only to get more clothes. After a while most of her clothes were at his place. Bryan drove her to work. He waited for her to get off so he could bring her home.

They went out together, they stayed home together, they read books together, and they took trips together. They never left each other's sight. Always together. Happy and in love.

She never thought she would ever love someone more than she loved Bryan. He couldn't imagine his life without her. He called her to tell her he closed on a house and he told her that he wanted her to move in. Briana quickly agreed to move in with Bryan. They began their life together from that moment.

When they first moved in the house Briana was so happy.

There was something special about that house. The energy felt good and they had plenty of room to fill it with whatever they wanted.

One day while they were cleaning the back yard they noticed two purple flowers blooming in the middle of the yard. There were no other flowers anywhere else around the house; just those two. They had never seen those flowers before and thought it was weird that only two flowers had started blooming in the back yard.

They took that as a sign that this union was meant to be and the flowers were a representation of them and the love they had for one another. They turned that spot into their special spot for talking or relaxing during the warm months in Minnesota.

They started off having lots of barbeques inviting all of their friends and family over to have a good time with them. That's how Bryan met Briana's friends Imani and Mercedes; and is also how Briana met Bryan's best friend Tre.

Briana and Bryan would serve alcoholic beverages and food that they cooked and prepared with love and care. They would sit around talking and laughing in the backyard until dark. Sometimes after dark they would go inside and get a game of spades, dominos, or monopoly going. Everyone would stay until late and then go home after a few games.

They really had a good time having outdoor barbeques during the spring and summer months in Minnesota. Once it got cold the outdoor barbeques turned into indoor gatherings. A little music, drinks, and a few friends would make an indoor get together just as fun as an outdoor barbeque.

They were all like family; however, Mercedes would

sometimes get a little too drunk and let her mouth get a little careless, which made Bryan feel a certain kind of way about her. Eventually Mercedes mouth caused his dislike for her.

Briana felt like Mercedes didn't do anything wrong. It was just Mercedes being Mercedes in Briana's mind. Bryan mentioned to Briana that Mercedes seemed a little wild for his taste, but he loved Briana so he rocked with it. But during one of their barbeque cook outs Bryan walked in on Mercedes having a Mercedes outburst and he was pretty much through with her from that day forward.

That day Briana left the backyard to go into the house to get some more beers out of the refrigerator for the guys. Mercedes and Imani were already in the kitchen fixing another plate of food.

Mercedes is tall with light brown skin; a little lighter than Briana's rich caramel complexion. She sported green contacts and long weaves in all different shades. Whichever shade she was feeling for the week is what she wore. This week she was wearing a platinum blond thirty-inch weave with a part down the middle. She like her weaves long enough to touch her butt; no matter what shade; curly or straight.

Standing there in her expensive black stiletto heels showing off her flat stomach, and part of her floral side tattoo. Wearing a black belly shirt that read BAD BITCH in gold letters. She has a tongue ring, a belly ring, and a small diamond in her nose. She once told Briana that she had her clitoris pierced as well and asked Briana if she wanted to see it. Briana declined the offer while laughing. "Girl you are crazy." Briana told her.

Mercedes is a stripper, so she is about that life. Briana and

Imani are not about that life but they don't judge her, they just let her be her. They have known Mercedes since high school so nothing she does really surprises them anymore.

Imani has gorgeous honey brown skin and natural hair that she would wear in twists sometimes. She mostly wore her hair in afro like styles. If she wore a weave it was usually cornrows or single platted extension braids that were long to her back.

Imani never wore much make up, and is very slim in body size even though she had a three-year-old son. She was one of those people that never gained weight no matter how much she ate. Imani had her baby while they were in high school and it seemed like she dropped her baby weight the same day she gave birth to him.

"Hey girl!" Mercedes spoke to Briana adjusting her large gold BAD earrings with her long black and gold polished finger nails.

"Hey girl! Hey Imani!" Briana spoke to both Mercedes and Imani.

"How do y'all like the chicken this time?" Briana asked them.

Mercedes smacked her lips. "What you talking bout this time? Bitch it's the bomb every time."

They all laughed.

"Yes it is delicious Briana, and who hooked up this red beans and rice?" Imani said.

"You know I did." Briana said proudly.

"Giiiiiirl. You did that." Mercedes said.

"Yes you did. Girl you got to give me this recipe ok?" Imani said to Briana.

"I got you girl." Briana said closing the refrigerator with her hip holding two beers in hand.

Mercedes put her hand on her hip.

"Uh why the fuck he got you running back and forth grabbing beers like you some slave or something? Mercedes asked.

"Shhhh." Imani said.

"Naw I am just saying why the fuck can't he get up and get it himself?"

Just then Bryan walked into the kitchen and by the look on his face they could tell that he heard Mercedes. Bryan played it off like he didn't hear Mercedes.

"Hey ladies are you all ok in here?"

"Yes." They all said in unison.

Bryan looked at Briana and asked. "Are you ok ma?"

"Yes."

"Are you sure?"

"Yes Bryan I am fine." Briana said softly with a smile.

"I love you." Bryan kissed Briana on the lips.

"I love you too." Briana smiled.

Bryan took the bottles of beer from Briana's hands and walked back out of the kitchen into the back yard. Mercedes smacked her lips and started taking a sip from her drink.

"Mercedes your drunk." Imani said in a stern whisper; grabbing Mercedes arm to take her drink from her.

"I'm just saying." Mercedes said pulling away from Imani.

Briana put her hands on her hips and then looked at Mercedes who was taking another sip from her drink.

"Mercedes I don't mind running back and forth getting stuff for him. I am doing what a woman is supposed to do for her man. You don't have one so that's why you don't know that."

"Whatever I don't want one just for that reason." Mercedes put her plastic cup on the counter and picked up her plate of food.

Briana just rolled her eyes at Mercedes and looked at Imani.

"Do you need anything else girl?" Briana asked Imani.

"No honey I am fine but thanks for asking." Imani said. She was clearly irritated by Mercedes.

They joined the guys outside. Some more of Briana and Bryan's friends came and joined them too. They were having a good time. Music playing and great conversation.

Everyone was sitting around eating, drinking and talking about current events. Tre rolled up a blunt of loud and was passing it around, even Imani took a puff or two when it got to her. They stayed out there until late in the evening, then, everyone started to leave.

Mercedes stood up to leave after she hit the blunt a few times.

"I gotta go Briana." She stood and adjusted her Capri pants and belly shirt.

Briana stood up to hug her goodbye. "Ok girl call me later."

"Mercedes make that ass clap for me." Tre said chuckling.

Mercedes started walking. "Hell naw nigga fuck you." She put her middle finger up as she exited the backyard towards the front of the house so she could get in her car. Everyone started laughing.

"Yea I got to go too, I got to get home to my baby." Imani

said standing up.

Briana hugged Imani and walked with Imani towards the house. She wanted to get back to the kitchen to begin cleaning up.

Later that night Bryan expressed his dislike for Mercedes. Briana defended her but there was nothing she could do. Mercedes had already put a bad taste in Bryan's mouth.

"What's up with your girl Mercedes?"

"Nothing what do you mean?"

"She just seemed to be coming at you a little harsh earlier in the kitchen."

"She just runs her mouth Bryan, she didn't mean anything by it, Mercedes is cool."

"Yea ok ma if you say so, she a little wild ya naw mean?"

Briana had to admit Mercedes was a little wild and outspoken sometimes. That was still her girl.

"I know she is a little wild Bry but she is my girl, my day one, we been friends since high school. She got my back, she is like my sister." Briana explained. Bryan left it alone, but he knew he wasn't feeling Mercedes at all.

Chapter 11

Briana

When Things Were Easy

Shortly after that night Bryan and Briana got engaged on their one-year anniversary. He popped the question over a candle light dinner at fancy restaurant he took her to. Of course she accepted the ring. With tears in her eyes Briana said "Yes Bryan I will marry you."

There was no question in her mind that she would marry Bryan. All he had to do was tell her when and where and she would do it even if she only had bells on.

Briana was so excited she called everybody to tell them. She even posted a pic of the ring and a life event engagement post on her social networking page online. She video called her best friends to tell them.

"What's up B?" Mercedes answered the video chat brushing her red twenty-two- inch hair weave.

"Pow!" Briana put the ring into her phone camera.

"Omg! Whaaaaaat!" Mercedes shrieked.

"Yes Girl!" Briana yelled.

"Wait girl I am at Imani's house, Imani! Come here girl!"

"What?" Imani appearing on the phone camera.

"Bryan asked me to marry him! Boom!" Briana put the beautiful sparkling diamond ring back into the camera.

"Omg! Girl! Omg! I am so happy for you! We have to get together and celebrate!" Imani screamed into the camera.

"Yes we do! My place this weekend engagement party!" Briana yelled.

****

The party was all the way turned up. They had drinks and food as usual, but this time they hired a DJ to provide the music.

Everybody was there. Bryan's people and Briana's people. Briana had more family there than Bryan because most of his family still resided in New York, but his brother and cousin were in town. They did Bryan a favor by driving his daughters down for him. Of course Imani, Mercedes, and Tre were in attendance.

Briana was so happy she was smiling and glowing. Bryan was happy and smiling too.

They couldn't keep their hands off of each other the whole night. Everyone admired their love and watched how they flirted with each other and danced and kissed. He would smack her butt every now and then, and she would giggle. She would kiss him on the cheek or rub his arm and his eyes would twinkle. They danced and drank and partied all night.

"Congrats my man!" Tre said to Bryan as they toasted in one of the videos Tre recorded that night. Tre posted the video to his social networking page tagging everyone who was there.

"Thank you Thank You!" Bryan said back smiling and clinking glasses with Tre, Bryan's brother, Bryan's cousin, and three other friends.

Another video showed Briana's friends Imani and Mercedes saying, "Congrats!" In the same video; Bryan and Briana were dancing and singing to each other.

The party didn't end until late that night. Bryan and Briana were so drunk they barely remembered what time the party ended. All they knew is that they had the time of their lives.

The next morning, they both woke up with hangovers. Lucky for them Bryan's sister in-law agreed to watch Bryan's daughters for the night since she was pregnant and too tired to attend the party.

That was the last time all of them really hung out. The last time Briana and Bryan had a get together at their house. That was when everything was good. Before the twins, before the problems, before the drama. When they were happy. When things were easy.

Chapter 12

Briana

Romantic Things Start to Fade

Bryan was never home. Seemed like he was always busy doing this and doing that. Briana was working a lot. It had been two years since the engagement and the engagement party and they still hadn't planned the wedding.

They really hadn't talked about the engagement. They hadn't really been talking at all. Not like they used to. People kept asking Briana when the wedding was going to be, but she didn't know. They were too busy and at the rate they were going there was probably never going to be a wedding.

Since Bryan's twin daughters came to live with them permanently, seemed like they never had time for each other anymore, except when it was time for bed. Briana spent most of her days at work and then home with the twins. Bryan stayed busy in and out of the house all day working.

Now, they drove in separate cars and worked in separate places. Briana picked up an office job while Bryan started a remodeling business. Bryan's business kept him gone all day and sometimes until late at night. Most of the time, if he was home in the day, he spent hours playing video games with Tre and blowing loud blunts. Little by little the romantic things they used to do started to fade.

Briana missed when they would cook together and feed each other. She longed for movie and popcorn nights, evenings out to dinner, or going out to the club just for fun. She really missed them making love and exploring each other's bodies with massage oils while candles burned and slow jams played in the background. These days they did none of that.

"Bri." Bryan said to her while they were lying in bed one night.

"Huh?" Briana responded sleepily. She had just started to drift off to sleep.

"Ma I miss you, seems like we don't get a chance to be with each other anymore."

It was like Bryan was reading Briana's mind. Briana wanted to tell him how she was feeling for a while, but she didn't know how to go about doing it.

"I know."

"You feel that way too?"

"Yes."

"Well why didn't you say anything to me ma?"

Briana sighed. "I don't know. I just didn't want to bother

you. You have been so busy with your business and I didn't want to put more stress on you."

"Look at me Bri."

Briana turned from lying on her back to her side to face Bryan.

Bryan gently grabbed her chin and said. "I am sorry; I will do better. You don't stress me. I love you. I will do better ma I promise."

Briana stared into his eyes. "Ok. I love you too Bry."

Bryan tenderly rubbed his hand down Briana's face and then he kissed her slow like he used to. He rubbed her back like he used to, and he made love to her like he used to. They woke in the morning and made breakfast together for him, her, and the girls. Everything was back to normal for just a moment.

****

Some weeks later a sharp pain shot through Briana's stomach waking her up out of her sleep. She turned over thinking it was just a dream. Another sharp pain shot through her stomach. She jerked fully awake and grabbed her stomach. *What is that?* she thought while she slid out of bed holding her stomach.

She walked quietly to the bathroom. Another sharp pain hit. "Oh my gosh. "she moaned. The pains felt worse than cramps. This couldn't be her period. Her cramps never feel this bad she was thinking, then she felt something trickling down her leg. She looked down. *Shit!* She thought. It was blood.

She pulled off her panties they were soaked with blood. She figured she should sit on the toilet because it was coming out faster than she could get to a pad or a tampon. She started feeling more pain. She didn't know what to do. *Shit it's a lot of blood.* She thought as she heard clumps falling into the toilet.

She looked in the toilet. She knew that this couldn't be her period. There is no way. Something was wrong. She had never seen clumps coming out when she was on her monthly and it was never this heavy.

"Oh my gosh." she moaned as another sharp pain hit she grabbed her stomach then decided to lay on the floor. She couldn't take it.

Bryan heard her and woke up.

"Bri?" Bryan knocked at the door.

"Bri what's wrong ma?"

"Bry I don't know." Briana started to cry.

"I am bleeding a lot."

Bryan opened the door.

"Oh shit Bri." Bryan said.

There was blood in the toilet and on the floor. He grabbed a towel and put it under her.

"It hurts so bad Bry." Briana cried.

"Shit ma I think you're havin a miscarriage, why didn't you tell me you were pregnant?"

"I didn't know Bry." she continued to cry.

"We have to go to the doctor."

Bryan helped Briana get cleaned up, then he took her to the

emergency room. The doctor confirmed it was a miscarriage and gave her some medicine. When they got home Briana climbed into bed. She was drained and wanted to sleep.

Briana felt so bad she called off of work so she could rest. She was in disbelief that she was actually pregnant and lost the baby. She had never been pregnant before and this was a new experience for her. Having a baby was not something that Briana planned for, but now that she lost the baby she kept thinking what could she have done to prevent the miscarriage.

"It's ok Bri. It happens, It's not your fault ok ma?" Bryan was sitting on the bed rubbing her back. She shook her head yes and then drifted off to sleep.

Bryan whispered in her ear "I love you." and kissed her on the cheek.

Chapter 13

Briana

What Kiss?

"Why you love daddy so much?" That is what ten-year-old Daisia asked Briana walking through the largest mall in Minnesota one day.

Briana and the twins were out shopping. The twins were in need of some new clothes and shoes, and Briana just wanted some retail therapy.

It had been a year since the first miscarriage and about six months since the second one.

"Be quiet Daisia." Dalila grabbed Dasia's arm trying to shut her up.

"Because I do, just like I love you two." Briana poked Daisia in the ribs playfully.

"Do you two love me?" Briana asked the twins.

"Yes." they said in unison.

"You better!" Briana said wrapping them both up in her arms and squeezing them extra tight. They all laughed.

The three of them walked into one of the many clothing stores in the mall.

"Do you think daddy loves you?" Daisia asked.

"Daaaisia" Dalila said in a low aggravated voice.

Dalila was trying to shut Daisia up but she wouldn't stop. Daisia shrugged Dalila off. Briana stopped walking and looked Daisia in the eyes.

"Wait why are you asking me that Daisia?" Briana looked at Daisia with a serious expression. Dalila looked down at the ground.

"Dalila?" Briana looked at Dalila with her eyebrows raised. Daisia fell silent.

"Daisia? Why are you asking me that?" Briana looked back at Daisia.

"Well daddy told us never to tell you but sometimes when you are at work and he picks us up from school he makes a stop to see some lady and they hug and kiss" Daisia said.

Briana's heart started beating rapidly. "Wait kiss? What kind of kiss Daisia? Like on the cheek?"

Dalila shook her head no. Briana took a deep breath. "On the lips? You two saw them kiss on the lips?"

"Yes." Daisia said. "Is this true? Dalila is this true? You saw it too?"

"Yes." Dalila replied looking down at the floor.

"How many times have you seen this you guys?"

"A lot of times." Daisia said.

"But Bri please don't tell daddy we told you please we are gonna get in trouble." Daisia pleaded.

"I won't." She hugged them both "Thank you for telling me. I love you girls ok?"

Daisia and Dalila shook their heads yes.

Briana was pissed but they continued to shop. She was trying to have fun but her energy was all off. She couldn't stop thinking about what the girls just told her. Then she realized Bryan had been turning his phone off every night when he got home. *Damn!*

Just then, she felt somebody's eyes on her so she looked up. Some brown skinned thick chick with blonde hair was staring at her and the girls but she quickly turned away when Briana looked at her. Briana saw the girl leave the store. *Why the hell was she staring so damn hard?* She asked herself without saying the words out loud. Briana bought a few things for the girls and then left the store.

Briana knew she was going to have to investigate what the girls told her before she could confront Bryan. She was so tempted to go off on him but she promised the twins that she would not tell him so they wouldn't get into trouble. Briana was so pissed that she didn't want to look at Bryan, but she played it cool.

Bryan came home that night, turned off his phone like he had been doing every night, and
got in bed next to Briana.

Bryan cuddled up next to Briana and said. "Hey ma." He kissed her on her shoulder.

Briana's body language was cold. It took everything in her

not to pop him upside his head and go off on him.

"What's wrong ma?"

"Nothing." Briana responded with little emotion.

"Well why are you acting like that? You must be on your period or something."

If he only knew the stuff Briana had swirling around inside of her head at that moment.

"No I am fine." She said.

Bryan kissed her on the forehead. "I love you ma."

She stared at the ceiling. "love you too." She said dryly.

Briana plotted and planned how to get into Bryan's phone. She waited a few days until she knew he would be distracted. The girls were gone to a friends and he was in the living room with Tre playing the game.

She walked into the living room. "Baby my phone is broke I need to call my mom, she is supposed to stop by and pick up some nutmeg for a pie she is baking for church."

"Here Bri don't be too long." Bryan unlocked his phone and handed it to Briana.

She knew she didn't have much time so she walked into the kitchen while scrolling through the text messages. She saw one that said *I am sorry baby I can't talk right now*, to an unsaved number. She memorized the number.

Then she saw a bunch of text messages in there to someone named Jersey. She didn't think it seemed suspicious but decided to read a few of those too. Most of them didn't seem too out of the norm. She couldn't tell if Jersey was a guy or a girl until she read one from a while back that said *So what are you going to do love? You can't have it.*

What? She thought. She didn't have time to memorize that number too so she made a mental note to find a way to come back to that one later. She could hear Bryan getting up out of the chair so she hurriedly dialed her mom's number to place a fake phone call thinking *I can't believe he doesn't erase his messages.*

"Bri what are you doing?" Bryan asked Briana entering the kitchen.

"My mom is not answering. I am going to just bring it to her." Briana said as she was disconnecting the fake phone call that she placed to her mother. She allowed the phone to dial the number but not actually ring so that his phone would register that she made the call.

Briana found a pen and a piece of paper in their bedroom to write down the number she had memorized. She stuffed it in her handbag and left out of the house.

She drove towards her mom's house but then figured she didn't want to go there to make the phone call, so she went to the hair salon she and Bryan usually took the girls to. The owner was her friend Sasha. Briana knew that Sasha would let her use the phone there.

The door bells chimed as Briana walked through the door of the salon.

"Hey girl!" Briana said smiling.

Sasha turned around from working on her client and said in a cheery voice. "Heeey Briana girl!"

Sasha put the flat iron she was using back into the oven, then she walked up to Briana to give her a hug. Sasha was a little older than Briana and always made Briana feel welcome and loved when she came there. Sasha had a nurturing, motherly kind of spirit.

Sasha's salon had about six stylist stations. Everything was black including the floors, accept for the walls. The walls were white. She had chandelier style lights hanging from the ceilings which gave it a look of elegance.

Sasha was the only one in the salon when Briana walked in. The other stylists weren't in yet. It was kind of early so it wasn't that busy in Sasha's salon which was perfect for what Briana needed to do.

"What you up to?" Sasha asked Briana.

"Nothing. I came to see how you were and set an appointment for me and the girls."

"Ahhhh how are those pretty girls?" Sasha asked smiling. She combed out a piece of her client's hair and picked up the flat iron after it cooled off on a wet towel.

"They are good; they are getting so big Sasha." Briana sat down in one of the empty stylist chairs. She watched Sasha flat iron the piece of hair. The hair sizzled a little and steamy smoke arose from the flat iron.

"Yes they are growing up fast. How are you?" Sasha asked looking Briana directly in the eyes. She was waving her hand back and forth over the piece of hair to help it to cool off.

"I am fine."

"Are you sure?" Sasha asked. Sasha was very motherly and

intuitive, so she could tell something wasn't right with Briana.

"Yeeees." Briana said laughing. Playing off her frustration and her real reason for stopping by the salon.

"Ok, so when are you bringing my pretty twins by to see me?" Sasha said. She set the flat iron back into the oven. She then fingered the piece of hair she just flat ironed to loosen it up, then, she set the section of hair in place with the rest of the flat ironed hair that she already styled.

"When is the best time?" Briana asked.

"Ya'll can come Friday around five does that work for you?"

"Yes ma'am we will be here."

"Ok I will pencil you in my appointment book once I get finished. I can't wait to see them."

Briana smiled. "Thanks!"

Then Briana said. "Sash my phone is not working can I use your phone really quick?"

"You know you don't even have to ask girl, it's in the back room." Sasha told her as she was reaching for the flat iron again to take it out of the oven.

Briana walked into the backroom to use the business phone. Sasha's backroom looked like a living room with black and white diamond printed wall paper on the walls. Black leather couches and a large flat screen TV mounted on the wall. She had chandelier style lamps in the backroom. There is a desk in the corner that had all the office supplies on it including a computer and the land line phone.

Briana dug in her hand bag to find the number she had written down back at the house.

The phone rang a couple of times before a female voice answered.

"Hello."

"Um I am sorry I may have the wrong number, what is your name?" Briana was fishing for information. She knew she had the right number.

The lady on the other line hesitated and then said. "Um my name is Carla, I am sorry who is this?"

"Carla, my name is Briana, I was looking for someone name Bryan. Bryan Tate. Do you know him?"

"Uh yes I know him. He is my boyfriend, what is this about?"

"Boyfriend? How long have ya'll been together?"

"Six months, but wait who are you? And why are you calling me?"

"I am Briana, Bryan's fiancé, we have been together for four years"

"Fiancé?" Carla asked.

"Yes Fiancé he never told you?

"No."

"So you have never seen his kids?"

"I have never formally met them but he sometimes has them in the car when he stops by to see me, how did you get my number?"

"I took your number from his phone. Have you ever been to his house?"

"Yes like once."

"Wow…Will it be ok if I call you back?

"Yes." Said Carla.

Briana hung up the phone extremely angry. If she could create steam it would be coming out of her ears and nose, and if she could create fire it would be coming out of her mouth. She sped walked past Sasha. "I'll see you on Friday girl."

Briana entered her and Bryan's house from the back door and called out to Bryan.

"What's up Bri?" Bryan walked into the kitchen where Briana was standing.

"Hey babe, mom says hi, I need to use your phone really quick to call her, she wanted me to let her know when I got home."

"What's wrong with your phone Bri?"

"It's broke it won't charge so it's dead."

"Alright we'll get you a new charger. Here."

Bryan unlocked and handed her the phone. He walked back into the living room. Briana pulled up Bryan's call log. There were four missed calls from Carla back to back; between the time Briana hung up with Carla at the salon, and the time Briana made it back home.

Briana tapped the last missed call from the unsaved number that belonged to Carla. The phone dialed Carla's number.
Carla answered. "Bryan?"

"No this isn't Bryan this is Briana bitch."

Briana got that line from a movie she once saw. She knew that it probably sounded corny, but she was pissed so she tried it.

"Bitch?"

"So you say you have been to our house?" Briana said loud

enough for Bryan to hear her.

"Yes." Carla responded with an attitude.

"How long ago would you say it was that you were at our house Carla?" Briana asked speaking extremely loud on purpose.

"A few months ago."

"Did you sleep with him here?"

"No but we made out, we couldn't stay long because he said he had to get his daughters from school."

Bryan entered the kitchen with a serious look on his face.

"Briana." He said loudly.

Briana looked at him but kept her ear and mouth to the phone. Making sure Carla could hear everything. She was leaning up against the sink with her hand on her hip. She was fuming and he could see it. Her nostrils were flared and her eyes looked wild.

"What Bryan?"

"Who are you talking to?" He asked with a serious tone.

"I am talking to Carla."

"WHAT?" Bryan stepped to Briana and snatched the phone from her hand. He looked at the phone to see what number it was and then put the phone to his ear staring at Briana with fury in his eyes. "HELLO!?"

"Bryan? What is going on!?" Carla spoke back in a very angry tone.

Bryan immediately snapped at Briana.

"What the fuck is your problem Briana!?"

"What the fuck is my problem Bryan! Who the fuck is Carla!?"

"Why the fuck would you go through my phone!?"

Bryan hung up on Carla and dropped the phone on the counter.

"Really!? You had her in our house!?"

"You shouldn't have been snooping through my shit Briana!"

"Oh My God Really Bryan!?" Briana grabbed her chest and walked towards the bedroom. She was in disbelief and felt her chest tighten as tears began to form in her eyes.

"Briana!"

"No Bryan leave me the fuck alone!"

"Briana come here!" Bryan followed behind her. Briana stormed into their bedroom grabbing bags, pulling clothes out of the dresser, and snatching clothes off of hangers.

"No Bryan you're a fucking liar and you're a cheater!"

"Where are you going Briana!? Would you just listen and let me explain!"

Briana kept stuffing things into bags. The tears started streaming down her cheeks.

"Just let me explain!" He grabbed Briana's arm with all his strength and slammed her on the bed.

Briana began to swing her arms and scream. "Fuck You! I Hate You!

"Shut the fuck up Briana!"

He mushed her face into the mattress with his hand. Then he placed his hand over her mouth and nose and said. "Shut the fuck up!"

NIA

Briana screamed into his hand. She couldn't breathe. He was suffocating her.

"You're not going anywhere you hear me!" Bryan said, his eyes wild and crazy looking.

The doorbell rang. Bryan heard it and let Briana go. Saved by the bell. She took a deep breath. She grabbed a shoe and threw it at him as he walked towards the door. Briana threw another shoe that hit him in the back and then a hand bag that hit him in the head. He turned around storming back towards Briana but the bell rang again.

"Briana you better calm down!" Bryan yelled towards the room. He turned around and went back to the door. Bryan swung the door open. It was Tre coming back from making a run for him. He forgot Tre was supposed to be coming back.

"What up my nigga?" Tre said handing Bryan some money.

"What's up Man." Bryan's voice sounded irritated. He was scratching his head.

Briana walked out of the bedroom and stormed past Bryan and Tre

"Hey Bri." Tre said looking at her as she walked past noticing how wild she looked. Then he looked into the house and saw that the house was in disarray.

"Is everything aight? Maybe I should come back another time."

"Yea I'll hit you up later."

"Alright Bruh Peace."

Chapter 14

Briana

My Life Has Been Empty Without You

Briana woke up to the sound of someone knocking at her bedroom door. "Huh?" She yelled out in a sleepy voice.

"Somebody is at the door for you Anna." Her mother said.

She started to tell her mother to tell them she wasn't there or she was busy but she decided to get up. She knew it could only be one person. She had been back at her mom's place for the past few days with her phone off so Bryan couldn't call her.

Bryan cheating on her had never crossed Briana's mind in all the years they had been together. She let him do his thing without ever questioning him. Now she wished she had. She wished she had paid more attention to little things like how he turned off his phone every night, or how he kept his phone locked.

Briana didn't pay attention to those things, so now she's back at her mom's feeling stupid. Most of all feeling angry and hurt about the whole situation.

She looked at her bedroom door not wanting to move. She didn't want to talk to him. She didn't want to look at him. She didn't even want to hear his voice. She couldn't believe him.

It pissed her off to find out that he was with another girl, but to have her in their house, and then have the nerve to bring her anywhere near the girls was disrespectful. Then on top of all that, to act the way he did and handle her so aggressively. Bryan was really bold for coming over to her mom's house in Briana's eyes.

When Briana walked out of the house after their fight; she drove around the city for about an hour in a daze, and then decided to go to her mom's house. Briana didn't really have anywhere else to go and her mom always kept her room clean and organized. "Just in case you want to come back." Her mom said when she moved in with Bryan some years ago.

When she showed up acting like everything was all good and she just came to visit. Her mother asked her what was wrong. She told her mom that she didn't want to talk about it and that she just needed a break. Her mother respected her privacy and left her alone. Her mom said. "Well you know your room is there if you need it, and there is some food in the refrigerator."

"Thank You." She told her mom giving her a weak smile. She was glad that her mom left it alone because she just needed some time to sort things out in her head. Plus, her little sister was sitting there looking like she couldn't wait to hear some juicy gossip, and she didn't need her business to be in the streets.

She never expected Bryan to ever act like that. The look in

his eyes was scary to her, it didn't look like him. She kept getting a flash back of him looking like a mad man standing over her with his hand over her nose and mouth.

She had never seen him look like that before. It was like it wasn't him. Like he was someone else or some possessed spirit had taken over his body. At that moment she didn't know that man. He wasn't the man she fell in love with. That wasn't Bryan. She didn't know who that was.

Briana got out of bed and went to the door. She looked through the peep hole and saw Bryan standing there. She should have known he would come there to find her. She shook her head and slowly opened the door.

"Bryan what are you doing here?" She asked in a whisper.

"Bri I have been looking all over for you ma, I was so worried."

He reached out to touch her and she pushed his hand away. He squinted his eyes at her. He was taken aback by her action. He wasn't used to Briana being so angry and standoffish.

"I need to talk to you Bri please." He whispered.

"For What?" she responded in an emotionless tone.

"Ma please give me a chance to talk to you?"

"No." She started pushing the door closed.

Bryan stopped it with his hand.

"Bri please allow me to explain, just give me a minute please." He begged with pleading eyes.

Briana stared at him. "Ok you have 1 minute."

She looked back and saw her little sister watching them so

she stepped outside onto the porch closing the door behind her. She faced Bryan with no expression on her face, and folded her arms across her chest.

"Talk." She said.

"Baby I know I fucked up ma, I know I did, I got carried away in the bedroom and I shouldn't have done that to you. You didn't deserve that. I was caught up in the moment baby and I am extremely sorry. I really am. You gotta hear me ma, I feel horrible. I will never disrespect you like that ever again."

"You done?" Briana asked.

He looked at her shocked. He wasn't used to this kind of attitude from Briana. When he didn't say anything she turned to walk back into the house. He touched her hand to stop her and she snatched away.

"You cheated on me Bryan. I have never ever thought about being with another man, and you cheated on me." Briana was serious and obviously still upset.

"No Bri baby I did not cheat on you. I swear ma. That bitch was lying ma. She was trying to get under your skin I swear. I have never had sex with her. She was my client ma I was doing a remodel job for her Bri. All she was; was just a client ma I promise you. Bryan said desperately. His eyes darting back and forth looking for some kind of expression in Briana's eyes.

Briana snapped at him in a loud whisper. "I talked to her Bry! She said she was your girlfriend! She said she has been to our house Bryan! She said she made out with you! And then you had the nerve to act crazy with me!"

Bryan continued to plead in a loud whisper. "Briana I'll admit to you; she was interested in me ok? She was and I knew it and I should have ended the job when I figured it out but I wanted the money. She has never been to our house. I have never kissed her in the mouth. I have kissed her on the cheek. And even that is too much I realize and I apologize baby. You have got to believe me. She knows I have a woman. She knows who you are Bri! She is just trying to break us up."

Briana took a deep breath and let the air out slow. She stared into his eyes searching for the truth. She started thinking maybe he is telling the truth. Maybe the twins thought they saw him kiss her in the mouth but he was really kissing her on the cheek.

Briana closed her eyes for a second; then responded. "Even if it is a lie you still handled me very aggressively, I have never been touched in that way. I couldn't breathe Bryan. I have never seen you like that and I am scared. I didn't know who you were and I feel like I don't know who you are right now." A tear fell from Briana's eye.

Bryan saw her soften up and stepped closer to her. "Baby I am sorry. I lost myself for a moment. I didn't mean to hurt you ma. I just didn't want you to leave. None of that should have ever happened. I will never do that again I promise." Bryan wiped the tear from Briana's face.

"Bri I miss you. I miss you so much. My life has been empty without you for the past few days ma. Please come home. Please come home ma. I will never let this happen again I promise. Give me another chance ma I love you."

He pulled her face to his and kissed her softly on the lips

and then continued to speak.

"You're my queen and soon to be wife. The girls have been asking about you. We miss you and we need you."

She hated him, but she loved him deeply. She was upset with him but she missed him too. She wasn't sure what was the truth or which parts were a lie. She really didn't have much evidence. All she could do was go off of his word or trust her intuition. She didn't know what to think. Something about it still wasn't right, but she loved Bryan.

A few days later Briana straightened her room and grabbed the few things she had with her. She kissed her mom on the cheek and said bye. Her mom said "The room will be here just in case you need it baby." She smiled at her mom. She shoulder nudged her little sister goodbye and left.

Chapter 15

Briana

Back to Normal for a Little While

Life at home with Bryan, Briana, and the twins was back to normal for a little while. When she arrived after being gone for a few days, Bryan welcomed her home with beautiful roses, champagne, and a bubble bath. He had also bought her a few expensive purses for apology gifts.

He stopped being gone a lot. He was more attentive. He wasn't turning his phone off every night. Some months had gone by and they were back to being happy and in love, but it soon all faded again. Bryan got back to some of his old ways again.

Briana noticed that he starting questioning her a lot. He started disappearing some weekends claiming he was at work late or with Tre. There were times when he wouldn't answer the phone. Some nights he would turn it off but tell her that it died.

Briana would be calling Tre looking for him. Tre would tell her he would have him call her right back but Bryan would never call. When she asked Bryan about it he would brush her off or get extremely aggravated and tell her she was tripping.

One night he came in late with Tre drunk coming from where ever they were. He claimed they were at the club. She confronted him when he walked in their bedroom. The conversation got heated and turned into an argument.

She had been sitting up all night waiting for him to come home. As the hours went by her anger increased. Every time she called and he didn't answer, her patience thinned. By the time he walked in the house she was at a peak level of anger.

It was during the winter and the twins were gone back home to visit their mom and family for the holidays. It was extremely cold outside and Briana had sat up all night watching the snow fall through the window waiting for Bryan to show up. She had been sitting in silence with her cell phone in her hand calling him back to back. He never answered.

Briana started screaming at him when he walked in their room.

"Where the fuck have you been!? I have been calling you all night!"

Bryan didn't want to talk, his explanation sounded shaky and Briana was pushing because she was pissed.

"Briana I don't have time for this shit! Bryan yelled.

"You don't have time for it?! Ok. Fine."

Briana stood up and started putting on clothes over her pajamas.

"Where the fuck are you going!?"

"You don't have time for it, well I don't have time for it either. You can stay out all night, so can I."

"You're not going anywhere Briana!"

"Why the fuck not!? You have been out all night!"

"Bri you're trippin!"

"No! I am fucking tired Bryan!"

Briana stepped towards the door and he blocked it. She stepped to the side and he blocked her. She stepped to the other side he blocked her.

She folded her arms. "Move Bryan!"

She pulled her phone out of her pocket to call one of her girls. He slapped the phone out of hand and it shattered on the ground.

"Fuck you Bryan!" She charged to get to the door. He pushed her back with all his strength. Her back hit the dresser and all the cologne bottles and perfume bottles fell making loud sounds as they hit the wood floor.

He grabbed her by her jacket and started ripping it off of her. "Let me go!" Briana screamed as she fell to the floor with him on top of her in a rage. Bryan kept pulling the jacket with one hand around her neck. Briana could hear the jacket ripping as he attempted to rip it off of her. Briana had her hands on his chest trying to push him off of her. Bryan would not let go. He was drunk, he was in a rage, and he wasn't going to let her leave.

"Hell no you aint going nowhere Bri!" He yelled.

Tre heard them and stormed into the room "Bryan man get off of her!" He grabbed Bryan by the back of his shirt pulling him off of Briana. Briana started kicking and punching at Bryan.

Bryan started yelling. "Get the fuck off me nigga!" His face red. He had white foamy looking spit caking up in the of corners his mouth.

"Nigga calm down!" Tre yelled.

Bryan yelled back. "This aint your business Tre!"

Tre managed to pull Bryan out of the bedroom.

"Naw fuck that I am not about to sit here and let you put your hands on your girl like that nigga! The fuck is wrong wit you!" He pushed Bryan up against the wall. "Now calm down before someone calls the police nigga!"

Bryan still breathing hard pulled away from Tre and walked out of the house. Tre went into the room to check on Briana. "Are you ok sis?"

Briana was sitting on the foot of the bed. She just shook her head yes.

"I am sorry sis; look you don't have to worry about him imma take him with me ok?" Tre said.

Briana shook her head yes. As soon as she heard the door close she leaned over and cried.

****

Tre stopped by the next day to check on Briana. Briana wasn't expecting to see his hazel brown eyes and sandy brown hair when she answered the door.

"Hey Tre." Briana opened the door and then stepped back

to let him in.

"Hey sis, I was just checking on you. I wanted to make sure you were ok." He stepped in and closed the door.

"I am fine Tre thank you." She said softly.

Tre being the light skinned pretty boy type with hazel eyes never seemed like the kind of guy that would be concerned about any chick especially Briana.

"Are you sure?" He said looking her over.

"Yes I am."

"I am sorry that went down like that sis." He said.

"It's ok Tre it's not your fault."

"I know but I just hated to see that happen to you, Bryan will be at my crib for a few days, let me know if you need anything."

"Sure and Thank you." Briana responded looking down at the ground.

Tre turned and left out of the door.

Bryan came home a few days later and the arguments kept happening. Briana would question and Bryan would get frustrated. If Briana pushed too hard for information, he would snap. She would cry and threaten to leave. Things would get physical and one of them would leave. So Briana stopped questioning him. She started doing her own thing.

Briana started hanging out with her girls more. Going out to night clubs, drinking, and coming home late. She never was really a going out type of woman, but the drama at home started pushing her to do things that she wouldn't normally do including talking to Tre.

****

"Briana where have you been?"

"I been out with my girls."

"Until this late?"

"Yes."

"Doing what?"

"Having a good time."

"Have you been drinking?"

"Why Bryan?"

"Because my girl is not supposed to be out this late getting drunk!"

"Oh really but its ok for you to stay out late?"

Briana took her jacket off showing off the short, tight, green dress with a plunging neck line she was wearing. The thin gold necklace she wore with it had a long chain that started at the neck, then, descended down the middle of her breast and connected to a belly chain. The necklace shimmered when the light hit it.

"What the fuck are you wearing Bri?"

"A dress Bryan."

"You wore that shit out?"

"Yes. So."

Whap! Briana fell to the floor and touched her face.

"You starting to act like that bitch Mercedes!"

Briana started to cry. "No I'm not." She whimpered.

"Take this shit off." Bryan began yanking at the dress ripping it off of her.

"Stop Bryan!" She stood up and started running towards the bathroom. He snatched her by the arm and threw her onto the bed. He entered her and began to aggressively have sex with her while she cried. He whispered in her ear "I am sorry baby, I love you."

Chapter 16

Briana

Briana's Mistake

Something about getting ready made her think about that night she had on the green dress. Briana walked around the hotel room she decided to stay in after leaving Malik's house. She looked closely into the mirror so she could see the spot where her face was bruised.

It had been a week since the fight with Bryan at the workplace. She was glad the bruise was no longer visible. All of her bruises had healed, but her emotions were still all over the place.

Briana decided not to stay with Malik, her friends, or her family. She didn't even call her girls or her family to tell them what happened that night. The only people in her life that knew about the events of that night were Malik, Bryan, and Briana.

She wasn't sure if the twins knew or not. Right now she felt like the less people who knew the better. Briana didn't feel like going over the details over and over again with her family and friends. The pain and embarrassment of it all was enough.

She checked herself into a hotel after that night at Malik's, and took some time off of work to be alone. She needed some time to heal from the emotional and physical trauma she experienced. Even though it was hard, she just wanted to forget about it for moment.

Tonight she was getting ready for Mercedes birthday party. Mercedes party is being thrown at a night club located in downtown Minneapolis. Briana was still feeling a little down but decided she would pick herself up and have a little fun with her girls. She hadn't seen or talked to them in days. Some cocktails, music, and dancing with her girls is the therapy she is in need of right now.

As she looked in the mirror applying foundation, she began thinking about the last time she had seen Tre. The night Briana realized that her and Tre's relationship had gotten too close. The night that Bryan almost killed Tre after catching them hanging out at one of the local spots in the city. The night that Briana decided she would never have another deceitful moment again.

****

Briana knew that Tre was coming around too much, especially when Bryan wasn't around. Briana knew that her and Tre had gotten too comfortable with each other allowing them to spend more time together than they should. She talked too much to him. She laughed too much with him, and she cried too many times on his shoulder.

Tre started caring too much about her and his feelings started to develop. He started to reveal the truth about Bryan's lies too her. Tre knew he was breaking the guy code but, Briana was beautiful to him and he felt Briana deserved better. He loved to see her smile and hated to see her cry.

He lost respect for Bryan after the first altercation he witnessed between Briana and Bryan. Which made it easier for him to not care about what he was doing with her.

Briana knew he didn't care because he told her. She didn't try to stop it. It felt good to have someone to talk to. Tre was an escape from her drama filled life with Bryan. Tre gave her everything that Bryan was no longer giving to her. She knew he was Bryan's friend but in her mind he was now her friend too.

There was the hugging, then there was the kiss. The kiss that should have never happened. The kiss that was so good to Briana and Tre they both thought about taking things to the next level. They knew they had crossed the line. Briana told Tre they could never do that again. They knew they were wrong but something about it felt right at that moment.

"Briana I love you Bryan doesn't deserve you." Tre would tell Briana. Briana knew that's he should have stopped it then.

Nothing could of prepared either one of them for the wrath that Bryan brought on Tre. The beat down that took four big grown men, two of whom were bouncers, to pull Bryan off of Tre that night and drag him out of the building yelling "I'll kill You Nigga! You Disrespect Me! I'll Kill You Nigga! Don't ever touch mine Nigga!"

Briana had to drive Tre the hospital and she felt so bad she stayed with him the whole night until he was released from the hospital.

Briana went to stay at Mercedes's place for a while. After several phone calls, tears, arguing, yelling, screaming, hanging up, calling back, threats, begging, and pleading, Briana went back to Bryan.

Mercedes didn't want Briana to go back, because not too long before all that happened, Mercedes saw Bryan at a concert with some chick. She took a picture of them and sent it via text to Briana with a message Who *the fuck is this Bitch*!? attached to it. Of course Bryan lied about it when Briana confronted him about it. He claimed it was his cousin that was in town visiting. Briana just left it alone. She was tired of it all.

Tre and Briana talked a few times on the phone after they were found out, then Briana changed her number ending all communication with him. She never saw him again.

****

Briana did a close to professional job on her make-up and hair thanks to instructional videos posted online. She danced around the room to the music playing from her phone. She looked at the clock and realized it was getting late. She needed to get dressed quickly so she could head to the party. If she showed up too late Mercedes would have a fit.

She put on a tight form fitted black and gold banded style dress and a pair a black ankle boots that stopped just above the ankle.

She topped off the outfit with a black leather jacket and long gold shimmer earrings. She stepped back into the bathroom mirror to put a little edge control on the edges of her shoulder length jet black weave that she had parted down the middle.

Briana stood in the floor length mirror on the wall and admired herself. She was looking good and feeling good. She couldn't wait to see her girls and turn up. Briana was ready to have a few drinks, let loose, and dance all of her stress away.

Chapter 17

Briana

The Party

The club was turned all the way up. The place was packed from wall to wall, and there was still a line outside of the club of people waiting to get in. The dance floor was packed. A bunch of people were crowding the bars ordering drinks. Photographers taking the night life pictures were set up in the back with the airbrushed back drops.

All the players and bougie chicks who were too cool to dance were lining the walls watching everybody else. A bunch of people were by the DJ booth posted up. Mercedes birthday party was in the VIP section where all the ballers and want to be ballers were.

The DJ was playing all of the hot club hits that had the people on the dance floor going. Imani, Briana, and a bunch of Mercedes other friends were all in attendance. Everybody was dressed to the nines.

Mercedes wore a red short strapless spandex dress. Her

nude skin was visible through the crisscrossed material going up the side of her dress. Any person that wasn't blind could see that she wasn't wearing panties or a bra. *Certainly Mercedes style*. Briana thought to herself when she saw her. Imani wore a simple off the shoulder form fitted knee length black dress with sparkly black heels.

Bottles of Ciroc and Patron were in Mercedes's section on ice. Everybody in her section were having more than a good time. They were turning up for Mercedes and she was loving being the center of attention as usual.

Mercedes and Imani were overly excited to see Briana walk in because they were not sure if she was coming since they hadn't talked to her. They all shrieked, hugged, and checked out each other's outfits.

The party really started when Briana walked in. Mercedes poured Briana and Imani a shot of Patron and then poured one for herself. They all put their shot glasses up to toast for her birthday. Briana said. "To The Baddest Bitch! Happy Birthday!"

They all swallowed down the shot in one gulp. "Whew!" Briana said rubbing her chest. Mercedes and Imani laughed.

"Happy birthday Mercedes we love you!" Imani said still laughing at Briana.

They all hugged and then started dancing to the music the DJ was playing. Mercedes poured all of them another shot. They all took the shot and continued to move to the music a little.

"Where you been bitch?!" Mercedes yelled over the loud music.

"Yea!" Imani chimed in.

"I have just been busy ya'll!" Briana yelled back over the music.

Mercedes looked at Briana. "Um hum laid up with that punk ass nigga of yours that I can't stand!"

Imani just listened in sipping on a drink she made for herself bouncing to the beat of one of the songs the DJ was playing.

Briana laughed and nudged Mercedes. "Shut up girl! Anyways Happy Birthday Boo!" Briana pulled a small gift out of her purse.

"Aww biiitch you always pulling out surprises for my bday! Thank you!" Mercedes hugged and kissed Briana on the cheek. Imani smiled at both of them.

"You can open it later!" Briana yelled over the music.

Just then the DJ starting playing their favorite song. A song by Beyoncé started blaring through the speakers.

Mercedes said. "Ah that's my jam! Let's go!"

They all headed to the dance floor. They were all dancing and singing at the top of their lungs with the other people who were on the dance floor.

Mercedes started twerking making her butt bounce to the music. Imani and Briana were cheering her on and dancing along with her singing.

All of a sudden Briana felt a hand grab her arm and someone yank her towards them. Her facial expression changed because she realized that she was getting damn near dragged off of the dance floor.

"What the hell!" She said then she saw who it was. Bryan

NIA

had her arm in his hands.

"What the fuck Bryan let me go!" She tried pulling away.

"Let's go Bri. I need to talk to you." Bryan said loudly.

Mercedes immediately reacted. "What the fuck is your problem Bryan!"

She charged at him. Imani grabbed Mercedes. Everybody started looking. People on the dance floor started moving out of the way. Briana didn't want to make a scene so she told Mercedes to chill.

"Let go of me Bryan!" Briana yanked her arm trying to pull away from him.

"This is my girl!" Bryan yelled at Mercedes and then looked at Briana

"I need to talk to you Bri." He was still pulling her off of the dance floor.

"Bitch nigga you got my girl fucked up!" Mercedes started charging towards him again while Imani was holding her back. Security noticed the commotion and started moving towards them.

"Bryan let me go I can walk for myself! Imani get Mercedes!" Briana yelled angrily.

Embarrassed that now everyone was looking and watching the scene they all created. Briana walked out of the club in a fast pace with her head down. She couldn't believe what was happening. Bryan's nerve to bring his ass into the club to find her infuriated her.

"This fool has lost his mind." Briana said to herself.

She hadn't seen or talked to Bryan since their altercation. Since nobody knew what happened and she didn't want anybody to

128

know, she decided to leave to save herself anymore embarrassment.

Once out of the club she kept walking in a fast pace towards her car. Bryan followed her out and caught up to her.

He grabbed her arm again. "Briana." He said. She snatched away and stopped walking.

"What the fuck is your problem Bryan!? I am not your woman anymore! How dare you come in there and humiliate me like that! I am convinced you are fucking crazy!" Briana yelled. Her angry eyes were staring into his.

"You won't talk to me and I need to talk to you Briana. I knew you would be here so I came."

"Why should I talk to you huh?! Tell me why I should fucking talk to you Bryan!?" Briana yelled.

Usually Briana would not yell in public but she was feeling the patron a little bit, and she was still furious over their fight. Bryan had to be mentally ill walking up in the club snatching her up like she was his child.

A group of people walking past started staring at them. One of the girls said "Damn." The rest of the group starting snickering.

"Briana stop yelling you're making a scene." Bryan said quietly.

"I'm making a scene!? You just damn near dragged me out of a club and I am making a scene!? And now you think you are deserving of a conversation after the shit you did!? Leave me the fuck alone Bryan." Briana started walking again.

Bryan grabbed her arm again more aggressive than the first time. "Briana please."

Briana stopped walking and looked at his hand on her arm and then back at him.

"Really Bryan! Get rowdy if you want to downtown Minneapolis where all of these cops are so they can take your ass to jail! Let everybody see who you really are!"

Bryan's eyes softened. Her words hurt him. "Briana I love you so much, and I know I fucked up ma and I hurt you and I'm truly sorry."

Tears filled his eyes as he continued to speak. "I don't know what's wrong with me ma, but I'm seeking some help nah mean. Seriously. I'm sorry bout the club tonight but I didn't know any other way ta getchu to talk to me. You gotta believe me ma I really am sorry." He wiped his eyes.

Briana stared at him with so much fire. "Yea you are sorry...Fuck you." Briana turned to continue walking.

Bryan didn't follow. "I know your mad at me but please don't be mad at the girls. They miss you and want to see you. Please allow them that Bri. Please." Bryan said to Briana as she walked away. Briana kept walking without responding.

Chapter 18

Malik

You Miss Him Don't You

Briana sat at her desk at work Monday morning thinking about the crazy experience over the weekend. She hadn't talked to her girls yet because she just didn't feel like talking about it. The embarrassment of it all was enough for her.

The security guard stopped at her desk with a delivery of a dozen roses. "These came for you." The security guard said.

"Thank you." Briana said and gave a fake smile. She already knew who they were from. The security guard walked away. Briana read the card attached.

Briana I am sorry I love you.

Malik stopped by Briana's desk. "I'm sorry flowers?" He asked.

"Yes." Briana responded.

Malik shook his head.

"So how are you holding up?" He asked.

"I am alright. Just taking it one day at a time."

"That's what you should do. Where have you been staying since you know you didn't take me up on my offer." He said smiling.

Briana smiled a real smile back. "I have been staying in a hotel. My apartment should be ready in about a week or so. Just trying to figure out how I can get my things from Bryan's."

"You be careful with that; do you want me to help you?"

"No."

"Alright. You down for some Chinese tonight?" Malik asked.

"Yes that's cool."

"Alright meet me at the spot over by the University of Minnesota campus in Minneapolis around seven pm."

"Ok I'll see you then."

Malik walked back to his desk.

After work they met up at the Chinese restaurant for dinner. Malik ordered tofu lo mien and Briana ordered shrimp fried rice and cream cheese wontons. They ate while they talked, catching up on all the latest. Briana told him about what happened at the club over the weekend.

"That man is sick." Malik said after Briana finished telling him what happened at the club.

"But he wasn't like that until I found out he was cheating; I don't know what happened to him."

"It was always in him; it just took the right situation to bring it out."

"Yea. I see what you're saying, he masked it pretty well."

"Most sick people do."

Briana took a bite of her food and stared off into space.

"You miss him don't you?"

She looked down at her food.

"Yes."

Briana's eyes began to tear.

"But most of all I miss the twins, my girls. I miss them so much."

She dabbed her eyes with one of the napkins that was on the table. What Bryan said to her the other night had been replaying in her mind since.

"I understand. Breaking up with the children is the hardest part and they are innocent in the situation. It's not their fault things happened the way they did. It will take some time to get over them, but you will eventually."

Malik rubbed her shoulder with one of his hands.

"Everything will be ok B."

Briana shook her head up and down.

"Thank you Malik."

"If you need me to help you try to get your stuff just let me know."

"I don't know. That may cause more drama but I'll let you know."

Chapter 19

Jade

Niggas Ain't Loyal

Jade slowed down the speed on the treadmill to a fast walking pace. She dabbed her forehead with her sweat towel, then she changed the song on her phone that she was listening to through the earpieces she had in her ears. Jay -Z's "Tom Ford" started playing through her earpieces. The song gave her a surge of energy that she needed to get through the second part of her workout.

She slowed the speed a little more on her treadmill to a slower walking pace allowing her heart rate to slow down. She thought about the picture of that girl in Bryan's phone. She thought about the night she snuck his phone out of his jeans and went into the bathroom.

She remembered how she sat in the bathroom listening to him snore while she read text messages to a girl named Briana who's picture he had saved in his phone. Bryan forgot to lock his phone that night.

There were text messages saying how much he loved her, and how sorry he was, and how he couldn't be without her, how much he needed her. She also read text messages from before that night to Briana calling her ma and baby, saying some of the same things that he says to her.

Jade text messaged the picture from his phone to her phone that night and then erased the text message from his phone.

Then she text messaged Briana's number from his phone to her phone and erased that message as well. There were some other text messages to some unsaved number but she was more concerned about the chick with the picture.

Jade was so heated after reading those text messages she could have slapped him out of his sleep right then, but she decided she would wait so she could gather up some more information about this Briana girl. Since then she had been playing it cool. Waiting for the right time to confront Bryan.

She stopped the treadmill and wiped sweat from her forehead and chest. She scrolled through her text messages and looked at the two pictures she had. The one she stole from Bryan's phone and the one her friend sent her from that online profile. Both pictures were definitely the same girl, and both pictures were the girl she saw in his phone that night they had the argument.

The night he stormed out of the house after claiming the girl was his cousin.

It had been a few weeks since the night she stole the picture and this would be like the hundredth time she had compared the pictures. She didn't know if she didn't want to believe it or if she was just afraid to face the truth.

She walked over to the weight machines so she could start her legs. She sent a text message to her friend who lives down the hall from her. Jade asked her what she would be doing later. When her friend replied "Nothing." She asked her if she could come over for a little while. She wanted her friend to show her that online profile of Briana. Her friend said she was cool with it. She finished her workout about 30 min later. After a shower and changing clothes she headed home.

Bryan had been hanging around a lot less lately since that night. She wondered why that was. What she didn't know was since Briana had left Bryan he hasn't had anybody to stay home with the girls, so he hasn't been able to get out as much.

Jade figured he was probably laid up with Briana. Just that thought hurt her beyond words. Jade knocked on her friend's door.

Her friend answered. "Hey girl! Come in."

"What's up Tish?"

Tisha moved in the building shortly after Jade. She is a full time college student. Jade and Tisha met each other taking out the trash one day. They have been cool ever since.

"Nothing much are you coming from the gym?" Tisha asked Jade.

"Yea you know I be tryna keep it tight and sexy."

Jade walked in and sat down on Tisha's couch.

"That's right, and you look good girl. I need to be up in there with you."

"Thank you; you can come with me anytime."

Tisha's flat stomach was visible underneath her oversized cut off sweatshirt that she was wearing with a pair of leggings. Tisha's body was naturally small. Weight management was not an issue with her. She just needed some toning, and a better nutrition regimen. People tend to forget that being skinny doesn't mean that you are healthy.

"Would you like something to drink? I got some wine."

"Sure whatchu got?"

"What do you like white or red?"

"I'll take whateva you got. I need it right now girl."

Tisha stood in the kitchen and popped the cork out of a bottle of Pinot Grigio and poured both of them a glass. She walked with both glasses in hand into the living room. She handed Jade one of the glasses and sat down on the couch next to Jade.

"What's going on?"

"Girl this man of mine" Jade took a sip of the wine in her glass.

"I think he cheatin on me girl and I am fucked up about it. I found a picture and text messages to and from the chick you sent me a picture of in his phone."

"Oh hell no, girl I knew it." Tisha shook her head.

"Yea and I haven't said nuthin to him about it yet but I am ready ta beat him and that
Bitch's ass."

Tisha sipped her drink. "Niggas ain't loyal girl." She said.

"Right .... Can you show me that profile you seen her on?"

"Hell yea let me get my tablet."

Tisha set her drink down and went back into the kitchen to get her tablet off of the counter. She sat back down on the couch next to Jade and did a search on the social networking website for Briana Taylor. Briana's profile loaded and they searched it.

Her online bio said her name is Briana Patrice Taylor, she is engaged to Bryan Paul Tate. They scrolled through her profile page. There were pictures of Briana and the twins. There were pictures of Briana with her friends and family. Then they saw pictures of Bryan and Briana, smiling, laughing, and hugging with hash tags Loveofmylife. There were pictures of their matching BPT tattoos. Jade and Tisha recognized that some of the posts were no older than one month ago.

"What the fuck." Jade said angrily.

"Uh uh girl, that's fucked up." Tisha said.

"I am ready to kill his ass and this bitch." Jade said and then downed her drink.

"You want a refill girl?"

"Hell Yes."

Jade continued to scroll through in disbelief as Tisha poured her another drink.

"I can't believe you haven't seen this." Tisha said sitting back down next to Jade.

"Girl I don't be online, I neva really got into this internet thing ya know, I don't like
people in my business."

"I feel you."

"Yo you know what's crazy, I swear I saw this girl and those twins at a store in the mall a little while back, and the twins looked a lot like him, but I wasn't so sure, so I neva said anything to him."

Jade downed the second drink in two swallows.

"You mean you have never met his kids?" Tisha asked.

"No girl, every time I ask him he claims they are too busy."

"Oh hell no, that's bullshit he's been playing you girl, I am sorry."

Tisha moved the tablet away from Jade and rubbed her back with one hand. Jade teared up.

"It's fucked up cause I aint from hea and I trusted his ass."

Tisha felt bad for her. Jade wiped her eyes with the palm of her hands.

"I gotta go girl."

"What you gonna do?"

"I don't know. Can you send me some of these pics from online?"

Jade started walking towards the door.

"Yes girl I gotchu."

"Aight thanks girl I appreciate it."

"Call me if you need me."

"Ok."

Jade left and went to her apartment. She was so distressed she couldn't sit still. When she sat down she was bouncing her leg. When she stood up she began pacing the floor. It was taking everything in her not to call him and cuss his punk ass out.

She remembered she still had a half of a blunt left over from when he was over the last time. She went into the bedroom to get it. She sat on the couch in the living room and fired it up. She needed to calm her nerves.

Jade fired up the loud blunt and hit it a couple of times. She choked a little and then began to relax. She turned the television on and started watching one her favorite reality shows. She blew the smoke in the air and laughed a little at the television show. The marijuana was making her feel more at ease. She needed to forget about all of what she just saw for a moment and the marijuana was helping.

She heard her phone vibrate on the coffee table. She didn't reach to pick it up. She knew who it was and she decided it was best not to talk to him right now. She needed a break and some time to gather her thoughts. Plus, Jade didn't want to hear the lies coming out of his mouth, nor did she have the energy to snap on him about his lies. So she just let the phone keep buzzing while she smoked her loud blunt and watched television.

Chapter 20

Jade

Jade's Man

Jade turned the rental she was driving into the parking lot of the mall. She decided to go to the mall that is in Bloomington but closer to Eagan. She didn't feel like dealing with the craziness in the big mall, so she chose to go to a smaller one.

She drove up and down the isles looking for a good parking spot. She loved to get as close to the front as possible. Tisha was supposed to accompany Jade for this retail therapy session, but she changed her mind at the last minute. Jade just wanted to get out of the house to clear her mind. She figured adding a few new pieces to her wardrobe wouldn't hurt.

She saw a parking spot right up front, so she swiftly whipped the Jeep she was driving into it before another driver tried to get it.

"Yea!" She said excitedly. She was glad that she wasn't

going to have to walk to far. She put the car in park and turned off the ignition. She clipped her wallet to her car keys and got out of the car.

There wasn't any snow on the ground yet, but it was a cold Minnesota day. Jade was wearing a cute sweater with a pair of skinny leg jeans underneath her waist length North Face coat, and a pair of low top wheat colored Timberlands.

She shivered when the cold air hit her. It felt so much colder in Minnesota than back home to Jade. She hit the car lock on the car key and quickly walked towards the mall. Retail therapy was on the agenda for the day and she couldn't wait to do some shopping.

She stopped in her favorite shoe store first. She tried on a couple of pairs, but she wasn't feeling anything really. She went to her favorite clothing store next. A few things in the window caught her eyes as she was walking in. she couldn't wait to get in there to try on some things.

She picked up a cute sweater dress, then she saw a pretty blouse that caught her eyes. She pulled the blouse off the rack. She held it up in the air to look at it. She was definitely feeling the blouse, now she had to find something to go with it.

She started moving through the store looking at the other clothes. She wanted to find something to match the blouse. Two women walked in the door and headed to the other side of the store. She glanced at them but kept shopping noticing that both of the women were very pretty.

She found a pair of pants and a skirt. She figured the pants would be a better choice since it was getting cold outside. Then it hit her. One of the girls is Briana.

Jade instantly got angry and her heart started to race. She thought *That's that bitch right there.* Her mind started racing faster than her heart. She had to say something. She couldn't let this chick just walk out of this store without getting some questions answered.

She hung the clothes she had in her hands back on the rack and slowly made her way through the store towards Briana. She made sure she looked like she was shopping and looking at the clothes. As soon as she got near Briana but not too close she checked her out. She was short and curvy but not fat. Pretty skin with nice hair. A natural beauty. *She doesn't look better than me though.* Jade thought to herself.

Jade said "Fuck it." under her breath. She walked up to Briana. "Excuse me is your name Briana?" Both of the women turned towards her.

Briana said "Yes um do I know you?" with a confused look on her face. The other girl frowned.

"Do you know Bryan?" Jade asked.

The other girl said "Excuse me but who are you?" with attitude and still frowning.
Briana said. "Why do you want to know?"

Jade ignored the other girl and said. "Because I am his girlfriend and I saw pictures of you with him online and in his phone and I wanted to know how you know him?"

The other girl said. "Oh hell naw this bitch is straight

disrespectful."

"Mercedes shhhh." Briana said looking at Jade not losing eye contact.

"Girlfriend?" Briana asked.

Jade looked at Mercedes and rolled her eyes.

"Yes girlfriend for almost 2 years." Jade said noticeably irritated.

Briana frowned. "Well I don't know how that could be because Bryan and I are engaged and we have been together for 6 years." Briana said and crossed her arms.

"Bri you don't have to tell her shit." Mercedes said staring at Jade.

"Chill Mercedes." Briana said still looking at Jade.

Jade said. "Well he neva said anything about you."

Briana quickly responded back. "Well trust me I never knew anything about you."

Briana looked Jade up and down.

"Let's go Bri you don't owe this chick an explanation." Mercedes said.

"I'm not talkin to you." Jade looked at Mercedes.

"Bitch but I am talking to you." Mercedes snapped at Jade.

"Bitch?" Jade's attitude started flaring.

"Yea that's what I said." Mercedes rolled her neck while speaking.

"Mercedes stop." Briana put her hand up in front of Mercedes signaling her to stop. She kept her eyes on Jade.

"What's your name?" Briana asked.

"Jade, Bryan calls me Jersey."

Jersey that's the name I saw in Bryan's phone a while ago. Briana thought to herself.

Mercedes started laughing. "This shit is a joke for real, let's go Bri."

Jade looked at Mercedes.

"Once again I am not talking to you." Jade said to Mercedes.

"I don't give a fuck." Mercedes said.

"Mercedes." Briana touched Mercedes arm trying to calm her.

"You a side bitch so stay in your place." Mercedes said to Jade.

Their voices were getting louder, so the girls working in the store started moving towards the counter where the phone was. They could see the tension and figured they might need to call security.

"Like I said I'm not talking to you." Jade said looking at Mercedes.

"And like I said I don't give a fuck." Mercedes responded.

"Mercedes turn down." Briana looked at Mercedes.

"Turn down for what?" Mercedes said with much attitude as she was staring Jade down.

Jade put her hand up and said. "Anyways."

"Don't put your hand in my face bitch."

"Or what?"

Mercedes smashed Jade in the face with the palm of her

hand.

Mercedes! Briana yelled and tried to grab Mercedes, but Jade had already started swinging. Jade hit Mercedes a few good times before Mercedes got a hold of her hair. Jade and Mercedes were swinging and punching. They fell to the floor of the store. Mercedes fell on top of Jade. They were both pulling each other's hair. Mercedes hit Jade a number of times in her head and face before Briana was able to pull her off of Jade.

"Mercedes let her go! They are calling security!" She yanked Mercedes by the arm and headed out of the store

"Side Bitch!" Mercedes yelled as they walked out of the store.

Jade got up and fixed her clothes. The girls working in the store ran up to her. "Miss are you ok?"

Jade rubbed her hands through her hair to put it back into place.

"I am fine thank you." She said.

She picked up her keys and wallet from the floor, then Jade walked out before security could make it to the store.

****

"Cedes what the fuck is your problem!?" Briana yelled as they were getting in the car. Mercedes was smoothing out her hair. "I was doing what you should've done." Mercedes shut the car door.

Briana slammed her car door closed. "You could've got us

put in jail Mercedes we are too old for that shit!" Briana started the car and pulled out of the parking lot.

"Look she's a side bitch period. Anyways I told you that nigga wasn't shit. That's the bitch I sent you a picture of a while ago I never forget faces."

"That was not necessary Cedes I can handle my own business."

"Um hum you're my girl and I got your back period. Now what are you going to do about Bryan?"

"I'm done with him."

"I hope you are. Don't be a stupid bitch girl."

Chapter 21

Briana

What's Wrong with Me?

After Briana dropped Mercedes off at home, she went home to her new apartment. She was going to call Bryan but she figured what for. There was no point. She knew she was stupid for back sliding with his ass.

"What the hell was I thinking?" She said out loud to herself.

She knew that she made a dumb mistake when it happened, but she got caught up in the moment. Briana wasn't sure why she still missed him after all the stuff he'd put her through, but she did. After receiving flowers every day, she responded to a text. Then a few texts back and forth turned into a phone call. A phone call or two lead to Briana stopping by.

Originally her visit was just to see the girls and to pick up some of her things. Bryan must have had another plan in store because that isn't how it turned out.

Briana told Bryan she would stop by after work. She knew

it would be risky going to his house by herself, but she knew with the girls being there more than likely Bryan would be on his best behavior.

Bryan knew she would be coming to get some things to take with her. He wasn't sure where Briana was moving to because Briana wouldn't tell him. To protect herself she felt that it would be better if he didn't know. Bryan didn't push for information. He just agreed on the date and the time for Briana to stop by.

Briana arrived that evening. She used her key to enter the house. After all it was still home to her even though she was moving out. She figured she would leave the key with him once she got all of her things.

Bryan heard the keys in the lock so he hurried to the door to open it. She walked in without saying a word to Bryan. Bryan welcomed her with a smile. Briana gave Bryan a weak smile back but didn't say a word.

The twins came running from the lower level. "Step mommy!" They were so excited to see Briana, they ran right up to her and hugged her. "Hey babies!" Briana hugged them back. She was just as happy to see them.

"We miss you!" Daisia said. "I miss ya'll too! How have you two been?" Briana said smiling from ear to ear. "Good!" They said in unison. Bryan stood by the door smiling and watching them interact.

Briana didn't know if they knew what happened, but she was sure they knew something was wrong since she hadn't been there.

"When are you coming back?" Dalila asked.

"Girls let me talk to Bri for a minute." Bryan said walking towards Briana and the twins.

"Aww." They said in unison with sad looks on their face.

"I know girls you will have some time with her in a little bit ok?" Bryan said. He wrapped his arms around both of their shoulders and directed them back to their room in the lower level of the house.

After the girls disappeared downstairs he turned to Briana.

"Hi Briana." Bryan said as he walked back towards her.

"Hi Bryan." Briana said.

"Can I have a hug?"

Briana hesitated and then she said "Yes."

Bryan wrapped his arms around Briana and gave her a warm squeeze. He wanted her to know that he missed her. Briana didn't reciprocate the warm hug. She lightly patted him on the back with one hand. She released herself from the hug indicating that she was uncomfortable. Bryan let her go and stepped back to give her some space. Briana turned to set her purse down on the leather chair in the living room. Then she turned back around to face Bryan.

"Thank you for allowing the girls to see you. They needed that." Bryan smiled at Briana.

Briana didn't return the smile. She nodded her head up and down. Looking at him made her feel many different ways. She wasn't sure which emotion she connected with the most at that moment.

"Well I know you came to get some things. You know where the bedroom is."

Bryan moved out of the way so Briana could make her way to the Bedroom. She pulled a few garbage bags out of her purse and went into the room to begin packing.

Briana began bagging some of her shoes and purses. She quickly realized she had more stuff than the bags could carry. She hadn't given much thought to how much clothes and shoes she had accumulated over the years. She figured that she may have to make plans for another visit to get the rest of her stuff, and the next time she would have to come with some boxes.

Briana was in the middle of beating herself up mentally about not coming over there fully prepared to get all of her things, when Bryan walked into what used to be their bedroom.

"The twins have been asking about you. They were extremely happy to see you." Bryan said while he watched her bag some of her stuff.

"I wanted to see them." Briana said as she continued to bag her things. She took some clothes out of the closet and placed them in a different bag.

"Would you like some assistance?" Bryan asked.

"No." Briana responded hastily.

"Ok." Bryan said and walked out of the room. Bryan walked into the living room and sat on the couch.

Briana spent a few more minutes filling up the bags. She tied the bags and headed towards the bedroom door to take her things to her car. She planned to stop back inside before leaving to say goodbye to the twins.

Bryan met her at the door way of their bedroom blocking

her exit.

"Briana I want you to know that I do love you." He said softly and sincerely.

Briana didn't respond. Briana stared into his eyes. Her mixed emotions rushed through her body making her heart beat at a rapid pace.

"I am going to miss you being here." He touched her face softly and pulled her chin towards him.

"So much." Bryan kissed her lips slow and tenderly.

A tear slid down her cheek and before Briana knew it she was kissing him back. Before she had the strength to stop, they were walking backwards into the room. Without pulling away Bryan continued to kiss Briana and shut the door. Briana felt like she had no control over what was happening. The kissing had taken over, and as much as she wanted to stop it, she couldn't stop it. Lights. Shoes. Bed. Clothes. Sheets. Skin. Kisses. Sounds.

When it was all said and done. Her bags were by the door. Their clothes were on the floor, and they were lying naked in bed after making love for an hour.

Damn! she thought. She started beating herself up mentally. *What the hell was I thinking. This shouldn't have happened Briana.* She sat up in the bed and began searching for her bra and panties.

"Where are you going?" Bryan asked yawning and looking at Briana in the dark.

"I have to go Bryan." Briana replied still trying to locate her under garments.

"Wait you don't have to leave ma." He touched her hand.

"Stay a little longer please."

He sat up in the bed and kissed her.

She could never resist Bryan's kiss. She felt herself slipping back into what felt like a spell. Briana wanted to slap herself for allowing this to happen. She couldn't understand how the same man who could touch her so violently, could also touch her so lovingly and make her feel weak.

Bryan used his body to lay Briana back down into the bed while kissing her. Bryan made love to her again as if nothing ever happened. Like the arguments never happened, and the violence never happened. To Briana it almost felt like the first time.

"Bri let's just do it." Bryan said to Briana. He was lying next to her in bed under the covers.

"Do what?" Briana was staring at the ceiling in the dark.

"Get married. Let's do it for real this time. No games. No bullshit ma. I am for real. I want you to be my wife. Let's just start over from the beginning. Clean slate. Leave all that stupid shit in the past ma and be a family. Me, you, and the girls. I am not happy without you. I need you in my life and I know I am capable of making you happy ma. I know I can treat you right. Give me another chance Bri. Please. Marry Me."

Briana didn't know what to feel. She felt torn. Part of her wanted to believe him and say yes, but part of her wanted to say no and run out of there fast before it was too late.

"Will you give me some time to think about it?" Briana asked. She continued to stare at the ceiling.

"Look at me." Bryan said. Briana turned her head to look

at Bryan.

"You mean the world to me, and I will do anything to get you back into my life permanently. I know I fucked up ma, but if you give me another chance I know I can and will be the man you need. I will never put my hands on you again. I swear to God I won't Bri. Please forgive me and give me another chance. Please ma."

"I just need some time Bryan to think. Please will you allow me a little time?"

Bryan sighed. "I respect that. How much time do you need?"

"I don't know Bryan."

"Alright. I understand. Take all the time you need ma."

Bryan kissed Briana and snuggled his body close to hers. Briana just laid there and let him hold her until they fell asleep.

Chapter 22

Malik

Free as a Bird

Briana hated herself for spending the night with Bryan that night. Briana was walking around her apartment thinking about that night wanting to kick herself for actually contemplating getting back with Bryan. Just to find out that he has been with someone else for two years on top of all the other things she had been through with him.

She took her engagement ring off and set it on her dresser. She sat down on the edge of her bed. The tears began to flow. She wished she understood why this was happening. Why did he have to do the things he had done? Why did he have to change the way things were? Why did he have to cause so much pain in her heart? Why couldn't he just be the man he was supposed to be?

Briana's cell phone rang interrupting her emotional break down. It was Malik. She wondered sometimes if Malik could feel her pain, because he seemed to always call, text, or show up when she was feeling down.

"Hello."

"What's up B?"

"Nothing."

"How's the new place?"

"It's cool."

"Did you get some of your things?"

"Yes."

"What's wrong?"

"Nothing."

"B?"

"Yes?"

"What's wrong?"

"Nothing."

"So you 're going to lie to me? Ok."

Briana was silent.

"Are you busy?"

"No not at all."

"I was out and about and I was gonna stop by. Is that cool?"

"Um. yea sure."

"Ok text me your address."

****

Malik made it to Briana's apartment a short time later. Briana opened the door and greeted Malik with a hug.

"Hey B!"

"Hey Malik!"

"You look nice." Malik said walking in the door.

Briana was wearing black wide leg dress pants, a belted black blazer, and a sheer cream shirt with a black bra underneath.

"Thank you Malik and you do too." Briana responded.

Malik was wearing an all gray Nike sweat suit with a pair of gray and white Nike sneakers to match. Malik's locks were long and loose which fell just below his shoulders. She could tell his locks had been twisted recently by how clean and fresh all of the parted sections were. She could see his scalp between each lock. Briana also noticed his muscular physique through the sweat suit.

"I see that you have been working out." Briana said as he walked in.

"Thanks. I'm trying. I realized one day that I ain't getting no younger."

Briana laughed; then she shut and locked the door. Malik walked into the living room area.

"Wow I like what you've done with the place so far." Malik complimented Briana while looking around her apartment.

"Thank you." Briana said with a smile.

Malik walked around admiring Briana's décor. Briana's nude colored couch and chair were decorated with colorful pillows. She placed abstract colorful art on the walls to match the pillows. The glass end tables and coffee tables compliment the furniture and the art. She decorated the tables with plastic imitation white calla lilies held in glass vase's.

"I really want to get some area rugs." Briana said.

"Yes that would be nice."

Malik had a small gift bag in his hand. He held it out to Briana and said. "This is a house warming gift I picked up for you."

Briana took the bag and hugged Malik. "Aww thank you Malik. You didn't have to."

"Open it." Malik said smiling.

Briana smiled and sat down on the couch. She pulled a small square two- inch gift box out of the bag. She opened the box and pulled out a Swarovski crystal baby bird.

"Aww Malik this is beautiful." Briana said softly; holding the small crystal baby bird in her hand. Briana looked at Malik and smiled. Malik sat down beside Briana. "I just wanted it to remind you to be free. Free from hurt, free from pain, free from drama, free from fear, free from limitations. Just Free. Free as a bird."

"Malik thank you." Briana leaned over to hug him.

"I know it's kind of corny but when I saw it I thought about you."

"It's not corny Malik its thoughtful, beautiful, and sweet." Malik hugged Briana back.

Briana's phone rang breaking Malik and Briana's hug. Briana picked up her phone and answered it.

"Hey Imani."

"Girl what happened at the mall today?"

"Um Imani I am kind of tied up right now can I call you back in a little while?"

"Yes because I just got off of the phone with Mercedes and you have to fill me in."

"I will, I promise."

"Ok bye girl."

Briana hung up the phone. "I apologize would you like something to drink?" Briana asked Malik and then stood up and walked to the kitchen.

"Sure, what you got?"

"Would you like to have a glass of wine with me?"

"Yea sure."

Briana open a bottle of Chardonnay and poured her and Malik a glass. She walked back into the living room and handed Malik a glass of wine.

Malik held his glass in the air and said "Lets toast."
Briana held her glass up.

"To new beginnings." Malik said. They clinked glasses and took a sip of their wine.

"So tell me what's wrong." Malik said setting his glass down on a coaster.

"What? Nothing's wrong."

"B you can't hide behind that smile with me."

Briana laughed.

"So spill it."

They drank wine while Briana told him about what happened at the mall earlier. She told him word for word the verbal exchange between her, Jade, and Mercedes. Then she told him about the fight. She purposely left out the fact that she had slept with Bryan not too long ago.

She explained how upset she was that it all happened, and

how Bryan had the nerve to be messing with some other chick for the length of time that he was. She also expressed how part of her didn't believe the girl Jade.

Malik listened quietly. He laughed a little when she explained how the fight went down. Briana poured them another glass of wine and offered to order some take out for them. Malik didn't have anything else to do so he was ok with it.

Briana ordered Thai food for the both of them, making sure to order a vegetable entrée for Malik. While they waited for the food to arrive Briana opened another bottle of wine, and turned on her television. They sat and watched one of the reality show episodes being repeated.

"How do you watch this?"

Briana laughed at Malik's question.

"It's entertaining."

"It's a bunch of craziness."

"I didn't use to watch it so much, but my twins got me hooked on it. Especially Daisia. She lives for shows like this." Briana leaned back into the couch. The wine was starting to make her feel a little sluggish.

"You slept with him again didn't you?"

That question caught Briana off guard.

"Huh?"

"Don't lie B."

"What made you ask me that?"

"I just have a feeling."

The doorbell rang. Their food had arrived. Briana ignored

the question and stood up to go and get the food. Malik had a way of reading people that was unbelievable to Briana sometimes. Briana paid the delivery guy and took the bag of food he handed her. She walked back into the living room and set the bag on the table. She went into the kitchen to get plates, silverware, and another bottle of wine.

They both placed food from the take out cartons onto their plates. Briana poured the rest of the wine from the first bottle into their glasses. She opened the second bottle and finished filling their glasses. Malik and Briana joined hands and said grace, then they began to eat.

"You're avoiding the question." Malik said continuing the conversation he started before the food arrived.

"No I just didn't answer it." Briana said before taking a bite of food.

"A way of avoiding."

"Ok Malik."

"You tell me everything else why did you purposely leave that out?"

"Because I didn't want you to judge me."

"I would never judge you Briana."

Briana set her fork down and looked at Malik.

"What's wrong with me? I mean why did I do that?"

"There's nothing wrong with you B, everyone makes bad decisions every once and a while when it comes to love."

"Everything just happened so fast. I got caught up in the moment and in his words." Briana said.

"When you love someone it's easy to forget the bad things and get caught up in the good moments you share with the person. Until the bad shows up again. He is who he is. That monster still lives in him. What you experienced will always be inside him whether its dormant or not. It's liable to show back up."

Briana listened and sipped some more wine. Malik took a sip and continued to talk.

"Look, when I was a kid, I watched my mother go through the same thing with my father. I promised myself that once I started dating I would never treat a woman the way that my father treated my mother. You're not the only one going through this. There are a lot of women out here going through the same thing. You just have to be strong and know that its ok to let go and walk away. Be an example for the young women who are experiencing the same thing. Show them that they can leave too."

Malik took a sip from his wine. He swallowed then he continued to speak.

"Especially the twins. You think they don't know or see what's going on, but they do. Be an example for them. The will respect and love you more for it later. And hopefully they will choose a man whom is unlike their father when they get older."

There was a moment of silence between them. They both took another bite of food.

Briana said. "You're right."

Briana swallowed the food and then began to cry. "Damn Malik I hate that this all has happened. I hate that I feel like this. I hate that I love him. I hate that I thought about going back to him.

I hate that I have to leave my twins. I hate that I am starting over."

Malik pushed his plate away and wrapped his arms around Briana. "It's ok B. What you go through in life will make you stronger. Whether it's good or bad. You learn from it and grow. But you have to move on. You have got to move forward. You can't stay stuck on what could of and should have happened."

Briana continued to cry while Malik rubbed her back. He rubbed her back until they both fell asleep.

****

Malik woke up first. He noticed it was dark outside and in the house except for the light coming from the television. He checked his watch. They had been sleep for a couple of hours.

Malik lightly shook Briana to wake her up. "Briana" he said quietly.

"Hum." She moved and then opened her eyes. She looked up at Malik's smooth chocolate colored skin. She stared at him for a moment, then Briana leaned into him and put her lips on his. She stared into his eyes waiting for him to kiss her back.

Malik was taken aback by her gesture, but he did not resist. He kissed her back. Malik firmly pressed his big and soft lips against hers. They both closed their eyes allowing themselves to get lost in the kiss. Briana slid her tongue in his mouth. Malik tasted her tongue while rubbing his hands through her hair. The bottle of wine had taken control over the moment, and they were letting the feeling and the moment take control over them.

Malik started rubbing his hands underneath Briana's shirt rubbing her back pulling her to him. Briana gently slid her hands underneath his sweatshirt and up his back. She lifted the sweatshirt over his head removing it. She looked at his muscular chocolate body and rubbed her hands down his chest. She began kissing him again while Malik removed her blazer and unbuttoned her shirt. He slid the blouse down her shoulders and off her arms. The blouse hit the floor.

Malik lifted his body up off the couch still holding Briana, then he laid her on the couch. He laid on top of her and began grinding his stiffness into her. They both still had their pants on. Briana wrapped her legs around him grinding back into him. Their breathing began getting heavy, and they kept kissing and rubbing against each other in the dark. Briana rubbed her hands into his sweat pants attempting to touch his manhood. Then Malik stopped abruptly. He moved her hands from his sweat pants.

Malik looked at Briana's beautiful face, light eyes, and her caramel skin glowing in the darkness. "Briana we can't do this."

Briana looked into his eyes. "Why?" She asked with a confused facial expression.

"Because B." Malik lifted up off of Briana and sat down next to her.

"Trust me Briana you are beautiful. What man wouldn't want you. But I respect you and love you enough to do what's right. You are not ready. You are still in love with Bryan and you need to get over that first. You need time to heal."

"But I started this." Briana stated. She sat up on the couch and reached for her blouse that was on the floor.

"I know. But I also know you are doing it out of hurt. I love you too much to let you do this." Malik put his sweat shirt back on. "Thanks for the food and drinks B but I think it's best if I go now."

"Alright. I am sorry Malik."

"No need for an apology."

Malik kissed Briana on the forehead and then walked out of the door.

Chapter 23

Jade

Jade's Revenge

The doctor walked back into the room. Jade had been sitting there for few minutes waiting for the doctor to return.

"Well Ms. Franklin I have good news for you. You are pregnant." The doctor said in a pleasant and cheerful voice.

Jade was frozen but she smiled at the doctor. "Ok." Jade couldn't think of anything else to say.

"You are about eight weeks, so you are in your first trimester. Your fight could of cause you to lose the baby, but the baby is fine, you will just want to take it easy for a little while at least until you get through the first trimester." The doctor told Jade while looking through some papers on the clip board she was holding.

Jade nodded her head indicating that she understood what the doctor was saying.

"Well how are you feeling Ms. Franklin? Do you have any

questions?" The doctor asked. "Um no. No I don't." Jade responded.

"Ok well I am going to write you a prescription for prenatal vitamins. Before you leave you should stop by the front desk and make an appointment with a primary doctor for a follow up visit."

"Ok thank you." The doctor reached her hand out to shake Jade's. Jade reached her hand back and shook the doctors hand.

"Take care Ms. Franklin you have a good day." The doctor left the room.

Jade sat there in silence for a minute and then began to dress. Jade was unsure of what she was going to do. All she was sure of, was right now wasn't the time for pregnancy or a baby. Not after what she just found out about Bryan. She couldn't believe that she had allowed herself to get involved in some mess like this with someone like him.

Jade drove home in silence thinking of all the obvious signs she ignored. Her not ever meeting the twins. Bryan not inviting her to his house. Her being shielded completely from Bryan's life and his family. A man who loves a woman is not going to wait until after marrying a woman to introduce her to his family.

Then she thought about the first pregnancy that Bryan made her abort. That thought brought a tear to her eye. She now understands that the real reason Bryan wanted her to abort that baby had nothing to do with the twins; it had everything to do with Briana. The fiancé he had been hiding.

After she got into the fight with Briana's friend Mercedes at the mall, she noticed a little bleeding and realized she hadn't had her period. She had been so lost in Bryan and the whole situation she hadn't been paying attention to her menstrual cycle. Jade usually stayed on top of her cycle. Suddenly she couldn't think of the last time she had her monthly.

The day of the fight Jade picked up a home pregnancy test from one of the local drug stores. The plus sign on the stick showed up more than clear. She called a local clinic to make an appointment.

This pregnancy caught Jade off guard. She was hoping the doctor was going to say that it wasn't true. Unfortunately for Jade it was real. There was a baby growing inside of her. She hadn't had any symptoms. Jade wasn't tired at all. She didn't have any morning sickness or nausea. She hadn't gained any weight that she could see.

She was disappointed in herself. Jade didn't want to be pregnant. How could she be pregnant by a man whose whole life had been a lie. The messed up truth is Mercedes was right she had been nothing but his side chick for two damn years.

After Jade took the home pregnancy test, she snapped a picture of it with her phone to send to Bryan. Jade changed her mind and decided not to send the picture to Bryan, nor did she call him to tell him about it. She figured that she would wait until after the doctor's appointment to confirm that the pregnancy test was right and now she knew.

When Jade walked into her place Bryan was sitting on the couch waiting for her to come home. She set the keys down on the counter after closing and locking the door. She made eye contact with him but didn't say a word.

"So you don't see me sitting here?" Bryan asked.

Silence.

Jade wasn't in the mood for Bryan's shit. She didn't feel like talking because if she started talking she might snap.

"What the fuck is up with you Jersey? I have been calling you. You haven't been answering my calls or texts. Where you been ma?"

Silence.

Jade walked to the kitchen to pour a glass of water. Bryan stood up and walked towards her.

"You don't hear me talking to you?"

Jade set the glass down on the counter and started walking towards the bedroom.

Bryan's phone rang and he answered it. He started talking on it while following Jade to the bedroom.

"Hello? Yea that's cool, what time yo? Aight. Yea I'll be there. Peace."

Bryan hung up the phone.

"Jersey?"

"Leave me alone Bryan."

"No! I wanna know what the fuck is up!?" Bryan yelled.

His voice escalating set Jade off. She couldn't hold it in any more.

"You wanna know what the fuck is up yo? Ya lies is what's up Bryan!"

"What are you talking about ma!?"

"You know what the fuck I am talkin about Bryan! Briana is what I am talkin about Bryan! Your engagement is what I am talking about Bryan! Your six-year relationship to that bitch that you never told me about! Your whole damn lie of a life that I knew nothing about is what tha fuck I'm talkin about Bryan!"

Brian was silent for a second. Then he said. "You trippin ma."

"I'm trippin!? I have the pictures in my phone! I saw the pictures and text messages in your phone! I've seen her page online you fuckin liar!

"Jersey chill the fuck out aight!?"

"Hell no I ain't gonna to chill the fuck out cause you had me fucked up this whole relationship! You could have told me I was just ya side bitch! I'm fuckin done witchu! Lame lying ass nigga!"

"Who da fuck is you talking to like that Jersey!?"

"I'm talking to you!" Jade pointed her finger into his face.

"Don't put your finger in my face ma." Bryan stood there. He was getting angry.

"Whateva Get Out Bryan!" Jade pushed past Bryan and quickly walked to the bathroom.

"Comere ma let me talk to you!"

"Hell naw nigga! I am done witchu SO LEAVE!"

Jade slammed the bathroom door shut and locked it. Bryan stood outside of the door talking to Jade through it.

"Jersey open the door."

"Leave Bryan."

"Jersey open the damn door!"

"No! Bryan I don't want to see you and I am done with this conversation!"

Bryan started wiggling the handle.

"Open the fuckin door Jade! And talk to me or I'm going to kick it down!"

"I don't give a fuck what you do nigga! It's over!"

BOOM!

Bryan kicked the door with his timberland boot hard. Not hard enough to kick the door in, but hard enough to startle Jade. She stepped away from the door towards the sink.

"OPEN DIS FUCKIN DOOR!" Bryan's voice was echoing through the condo

BOOM!

Bryan kicked the door harder than the last time.

"BRYAN STOP! LEAVE!" Jade yelled.

"OPEN THE DOOR JADE!"

"NO!"

BOOM!

The door shook

"ALRIGHT BRYAN!"

Bryan stopped kicking the door.

"I will open it if you calm down."

"Alright I am calm now open it."

Jade unlocked the door. As soon as she opened the door, Bryan snatched her up by her shirt and slammed her up against the wall.

"What is wrong with you?! Huh?!"

"Let me go. I am pregnant Bryan." Tears began to fall from Jade's eyes.

"What?"

"I am pregnant with your child again Bryan and I aint nothin but ya side bitch."

Bryan let go of Jade and stepped backwards away from her.

"Shit ma, I'm sorry. I am sorry ok?"

Jade stood there up against the wall wiping her tears. She had never cried in front of Bryan before. He wasn't sure how to react.

"When did you find out?"

"The other day."

Silence.

"I just came back from seein a doctor. I'm eight weeks."

"Shit Jade I am sorry."

Bryan reached out to touch her shoulder. Jade sort of flinched when she saw him reach for her. His facial expression showed his shock by her reaction.

"Ma look I am not going to hurt you ok? I love you."

"I love you too Bryan but this shit aint right.

"Well what do you want to do ma?"

"I don't know."

Bryan looked at his watch and noticed that he was running late.

"Damn Jade I gotta go. Can we talk about this later please?"

"Um Hum." Jade replied looking down at the floor.

"Aight listen I love you. Ok?"

Jade nodded her head up and down. Bryan kissed her on the forehead and left.

Jade locked the door behind Bryan and sat down on the couch. She made a few phone calls and then fell asleep.

****

She woke up to the sound of her phone ringing.

"Yea?"

"Hey ma, I'll be there in five minutes ok?"

"Aight."

Jade was so exhausted she stayed on the couch. She heard Bryan's keys unlocking the door but didn't move. She was too drained. She had never seen Bryan act like that before. It totally caught her off guard and she wasn't sure if that was the same Bryan that was about to walk through the door. She didn't have the energy for it if it was.

"Jersey?"

"I am on the couch Bryan."

"Hey. Are you ok?" Bryan spoke to Jade as he approached the couch she was lying on.

"Yea."

"I am sorry about earlier ma."

"Ok."

Bryan sat down on the couch by Jade's feet. He picked her feet up and put them on his lap. Jade sat up on the couch and faced him.

"So what do you want to do about this baby?" Bryan asked.

"I don't know."

"Well I don't think we should keep it. It just aint the time."

"That's what you said the last time."

Bryan didn't respond.

"So you're just gonna skip ova everything else to tell me to get rid of our baby, and just ignore the fact that I know about Briana?"

"I don't want to talk about that."

"Don't you think you owe me some kind of explanation?"

Bryan sighed.

"What for Jersey? I love you and that's all that matters."

Jade chuckled in disbelief.

"Are you serious? I believed everything you told me and I am lookin stupid. Now you're asking me to get rid of anotha baby Bryan?"

Bryan sighed.

"Look ma I am not a perfect man. I am not. I know I fucked up and I am sorry. I met you when me and Briana were going through some things and I got selfish. I can't take it back. I do love and care for you deeply babe."

"No you don't, cause if you did you wouldn't have lied."

Jade started to cry

"Please don't cry Jade."

"Fuck Bryan I fuckin hate you right now."

"I am sorry ma."

"What am I supposed to do now Bryan?"

Jade wiped her tears.

"That shit between me and Briana is dead. I swear Jersey. I

want to be with you. I am going to introduce you to the twins, I am going to move you in the house so that we can be together every day. Ok?"

Jade didn't respond. She wanted to tell him about the confrontation at the mall with Briana, but she decided against it. She sat there in silence. He rubbed her face and kissed her on the lips.

"A baby will just confuse things right now babe ok?

"Aight Bryan."

"Do you forgive me?"

"Not yet."

"Alright I deserve that. Set the appointment and I will take care of the money."

"Ok."

"Let's go to bed ma."

Jade follow him to the bedroom. She allowed him to make love to her before they fell asleep. The whole time they made love she felt stupid. She couldn't believe that she had allowed herself to fall so deep in love with Bryan.

Bryan left early the next morning. After he left Jade got out of bed and began to pack her things. She packed everything she could fit in two large suit cases and one carry-on bag. She packed the rest of her stuff in a box she kept from something she ordered online.

She put everything in the rental she was driving and returned to the condo. She sat on the couch to send a text.
He tells me that he loves me and that I will be his wife one day. I know he says the same thing to you.

She sent the text to Briana's number. Then she sent the picture of her positive pregnancy test with a message attached to Briana.

I'm keeping it -Jade (Jersey)

Jade did one more look around the condo to make sure she got everything. She left the pregnancy test and a note on the counter for Bryan.

On the way to the airport she mailed the box to her mom's house back home. Jade dropped the rental car off at the place Bryan got it from. She took a cab from the rental car lot to the airport. During the ride to the airport Jade thought about everything that happened. She thought about how naïve she was dealing with Bryan. Having an abortion for him. Tattooing his name on her back. She had been completely lost in love with him.

She thought about how stupid she must have looked confronting his fiancé that she knew nothing about. Lesson learned. Jade was saying goodbye to Minnesota and Bryan and all of the baggage that came with him. Jade was taking herself and her baby home.

Chapter 24

Malik

Friends

Malik heard a knock at the door so he stood up from the couch to answer it. His house shoes slid across the floor as he walked to the door. He looked through the peep hole and saw Briana. He unlocked and opened the door.

Briana handed him a bag. "I think this belongs to you." She said handing him the bag. Malik took the bag from her and looked in it.

What is it?" He asked with a confused look on his face.

"It is the sweat suit you let me wear the night I was over here." Briana replied smiling.

Malik laughed.

"You didn't have to give this back to me B."

Briana giggled.

"I know but I had to find a reason to come over here and

talk to you. Are you busy? I am sorry I showed up unannounced."

Malik opened the door wider.

"It's ok B come in."

He stepped to the side so that Briana could walk in.

"How did you get in the building?" Malik asked Briana.

Briana giggled. She said. "I have my ways."

Briana walked in and took her boots off at the door. It had been snowing outside and she didn't want to track water through his apartment.

"So how are you? I haven't seen you much at work lately."

Briana unzipped her coat and removed her gloves. Malik took Briana's coat after she removed it and hung it in the closet that is located by the door.

"I have been good B and you?"

Briana adjusted the form fitted, knee length, brown sweater she was wearing over a pair of black leggings and begin walking towards the couch.

"I can't complain."

Briana sat down on the couch. Malik walked over to the couch and sat down next to Briana.

"So what's up B?"

"I just wanted to come over here and apologize for coming on to you when you were at my house. You were right. I wasn't in a good head space and I put you in an uncomfortable position. I am sorry Malik."

"You don't have to apologize Briana."

"Yes I do because you have been distant for the past couple of weeks."

"Briana I am as responsible for what happened as you are. I figured it would be best to let things cool down between us before we both did something we may later regret."

Briana nervously rubbed her hands together. She didn't know why she was so nervous, but her hands were sweaty.

"So are we cool?" She asked.

Malik put his hands on hers.

"Yes Briana. Why are you so nervous? Calm down it's just me." Malik laughed.

Briana smiled.

Malik picked up his DVD remote and pressed play. He paused the movie he was watching to answer the door when Briana came.

Briana asked. "What are you watching?"

"Malcolm X."

"The Spike Lee movie?"

"Yes this is one of my favorite movies."

"I have never seen this movie."

"What? How is that possible?"

"I don't know." Briana laughed.

"This movie is genius. It's a classic. Denzel Washington did his thing in this movie."

Malik stood up.

"Are you hungry?" He asked Briana.

He walked towards the kitchen.

"A little what you got?"

"A little something."

He opened the refrigerator door searching for something to eat. He pulled out a bowl of left over pasta he made the night before.

"How does pasta sound?"

"Sounds good to me."

Briana started watching some of the movie while Malik warmed up the pasta for the both them.

"So what's up with Bryan? Have you talked to him?"

"Yes I talked to him."

"What did he say? Did you ask him about the girl Jade?"

"No. He called asking me to come move back in with him, and telling me how much he loved me and cared about me, and how bad he wants to marry me."

"Uh huh."

"Same ole. Same ole."

"So why didn't you ask him about Jade?"

"I wasn't ready to hear him lie some more."

"Right."

"You know what's crazy Malik? The girl Jade text me to tell me that he had been promising to marry her, and guess what else?

"What?'

"She text me a picture of a pregnancy test that I guess she took and it was positive and she said she was keeping it."

"Get the fuck out of here." Malik said and then laughed.

Briana laughed a little and then said. "You know what else?

The girl Jade, is the same girl I saw at the mall that day that I was shopping with the twins, the same girl that Mercedes sent me a pic of that Bryan claimed was his cousin, and the same girl that he had saved in his phone under the name Jersey."

"Wow." Malik raised his eyebrows.

"I am sure if I do talk to him he is going to act like he doesn't know what I am talking about. Or, he is gonna tell me some crazy lie about how crazy the bitch is, and how she has been stalking him. Or that he never messed with her, or she was just his friend, or how she is lying about the whole entire thing to trap him because he doesn't want to be with her."

Malik laughed again. He scooped the pasta from the pan onto the two plates he set out for them.

"You can tell I've heard it all before huh?"

"That man is crazy." Malik said.

Briana shook her head side to side. Rolled her eyes and leaned back into the couch. She stared up at the ceiling. "Yea he is." She said.

"So how do you feel about it?"

"I don't know yet."

Malik pulled a couple of forks out of the dish washer.

"What would you like to drink?"

"Water is fine."

Malik poured them both a glass of water. Briana stood up and walked to the kitchen to get the plates of pasta. She picked up the plates and turned to walk back into the living room. Malik followed with the glasses of water.

"So what do you got planned this weekend?" Malik asked as they sat down on the couch.

Briana set their plates down on the coffee table in front of them. "Nothing why?"

"Because I got two tickets to the Jill Scott concert. Do you want to go?"

"Yes!" Briana said excitedly.

"Cool." Malik smiled.

They ate and finished watching Malcom X.

Chapter 25

Briana

Girl's Night

"**M**utha Fuckas better recognize who I am! I'm Mercedes Bitch!" Briana and Imani laughed out loud. Mercedes was wearing high waist stone washed jeans and a crop sweatshirt that read "Celfie" across it. She was standing up telling them a story about something that happened at the club she works at.

Imani was laying on Briana's carpeted living room floor. Briana was sitting on the couch. All three of them had glasses of wine in their hands.

"Mercedes you are crazy!" Briana said laughing.

"I just don't play with these niggas, somebody better ask about me!"

Imani and Briana laughed.

Briana stood up and walked into the kitchen to get another

bottle of wine.

"I hear you girl." She said to Mercedes.

"Your ass is looking really juicy in that sweater dress you got on girl." Mercedes said to Briana.

"Really?" Briana said to Mercedes. Briana poked her butt out and looked back attempting to look at it.

"Um hum look like it got a little thicker."

"It does." Imani said looking at Briana poking her butt out.

"Well let me make it clap for ya'll." Briana started bouncing her butt.

Imani and Mercedes laughed.

"Please stop girl you don't know what you are doing! You're not about that life!" Mercedes said laughing.

Then they all laughed. Briana walked back into the living room with a bottle of Sauvignon Blanc.

"Well please teach me so I can do it for my next man."

"Oh so you and Bryan are over huh?" Mercedes asked.

"Yes." Briana responding not really wanting to talk about it.

"So what happened after I beat that side bitch's ass at the mall?"

"I haven't talked to him about it yet." Briana said and took a sip of her wine.

"Are you going to talk to him?" Imani asked.

"I don't know." Briana said staring at the crystal baby bird that Malik bought her. It was on the coffee table.

"You should let me confront his punk ass I'll send him back

home crying to his mama." Mercedes said.

Briana lightly chuckled.

Imani noticed that Briana seemed uncomfortable so she changed the subject.

"On another note my baby daddy still on bullshit."

"What's up with him?" Mercedes asked.

"Girl he still in these streets talking about he's hustling all day, but he still doesn't have any money to help me pay a bill or buy our son some new clothes and shoes."

Briana shook her head and took a sip of her wine.

"The other day he had the nerve to ask me for some money ya'll."

"That is messed up." Briana said.

Mercedes said. "Oh Hell No!"

"Right I am taking care of your son basically by myself and you have the nerve to be asking me for some money. Imani said. She took a sip from her glass of wine.

"See y'all are the reason that I am single." Mercedes said.

"For real there's too many Fuck niggas out here. I don't have the time. Give me what I need and get the fuck on straight up."

They all laughed.

Briana's phone buzzed. She picked it up and read the text message from Malik telling her that he hoped she was having a good night. Briana sent a text message back saying that she was and she hoped that he was too. Malik text her back to say that he was thinking about her. Briana smiled. Text Malik back a few smiley faces and set the phone down.

"Who was that? Who got you smiling like that?" Mercedes asked.

"Huh?"

"Don't huh me bitch I saw you!"

Briana laughed.

"He is just my friend."

"Does your friend have a name?"

"His name is Malik." Briana said shyly.

Imani smiled and sat up adjusting her leggings.

"Ooooh Malik huh?" Imani said.

"And what is Malik doing to make you smile like that? Is he giving you the business?"

Briana giggled and blushed.

"No. he is just my friend and that is all."

"Where did you meet him?" Imani asked.

"We work together."

"Oh that's nice." Imani said.

"Aw shit it's an office love affair!" Mercedes said.

"Cedes he is just my friend." Briana laughed.

"Well I hope he ain't nothing like Bryan." Mercedes laughed.

"He's not." Briana set her cell phone on the coffee table.

"Um hum ok." Mercedes said and then changed the subject.

"Let me tell y'all about this lame ass nigga I went on a date with." Mercedes said.

Briana and Imani laughed.

"What happened girl?" Briana asked.

Mercedes began to tell them about the date. Imani and Briana listened and laughed while Mercedes told her animated story.

Night hours turned to early morning hours and they were all tipsy and sleepy. They were all lying down barely able to keep their eyes open. Briana brought blankets and pillows out of the bedroom for everybody. They laid back and chilled listening to Pandora until they all fell asleep.

Chapter 26

Briana

It's Over

"top Bryan."

"Why?"

"Because."

"Because what Bri?"

Briana was back at Bryan's house again. The house they once shared. The house that held so many happy memories of them, but also held so many bad memories too. He'd been calling her again begging her to come over to see the twins, and once again he was trying to trap her.

She stopped by again to see Daisia and Dalila. She was trying so hard to let them go but she was having a difficult time with it. It didn't help that the twins called a couple of times too. Briana wondered if Bryan put them up to it. Nonetheless Briana agreed to another visit. Of course Bryan was going to try to use that to his advantage.

He was leaning in for a kiss and Briana put her hand up to block him. She wasn't in the mood to play the games with Bryan this time.

"Why are you doing that Bri?"

"I just don't want a kiss Bryan."

"I miss you Bri, and the girls miss you."

"Um Hum."

"I just want us to be a family again."

"You always say that Bryan."

"I am serious Bri, I am ready to marry you right now. Today. Let's go and get married today ma."

Hearing that infuriated Briana. She knew that Bryan has to know by now, that Briana found out about Jade and the baby. She could feel the anger start to burn in her stomach as she looked Bryan in the eyes. *He can't really be serious.* Briana thought to herself. She stood there silent for a moment trying to keep her composure.

It had been several weeks since the mall incident with Jade, and Briana hadn't said anything to Bryan about it. Briana wanted to see how long Bryan was going to keep up with his game.

She hadn't seen Bryan since before the mall incident, but she had talked to him. Looking at him stand there in her face, and act like nothing ever happened, was itching her nerves something serious. Briana felt like she was about to explode.

"Don't say that." Briana responded with a stern voice.

"Why Bri? I mean it." Bryan said with sincere eyes.

"No you don't Bry." Briana said with a straight face.

Bryan looked at Briana with shock in his eyes. Briana continued to give him direct eye contact. She stared into his eyes searching for truth. There wasn't any. Briana began to talk before Bryan could say another word.

"It amazes me how you can stand there and be so deceitful with a straight face. When you know damn well that you have been maintaining a relationship with another woman for two years behind my back."

Her voice was low and maintained and her words were deliberate. She never lost eye contact with Bryan the whole time she spoke.

"That's not true Bri."

"It's Not?" Briana asked sarcastically.

"No."

"Really Bryan?"

Briana said as her voice started to quiver. The tears began to form in her eyes. The lie made her feel weak. It was unbelievable that this was the man she has been in love with for six almost seven years; standing there in what used to be their kitchen; bold face lying to her again.

"Excuse me." Briana said calmly. Her chest was starting to feel tight, and Briana felt like she was going to snap.

Briana walked around Bryan through the doorway of the kitchen, through the dining room, towards the living room so she could leave through the front door. She needed to get away from him. She couldn't take it anymore.

Bryan called after her while following her through the house.

"Briana that is a lie. You know bitches lie."

Briana stopped walking and faced Bryan.

"Bitches lie? That's all you can say Bryan?"

Bryan put his hands in his pockets.

"I have given six years of my life to you. I have dealt with your shit. Your lies. Your cheating. Your abuse. I have had two miscarriages and you have the nerve to stand here and lie when I met the bitch. And I have a picture of her positive pregnancy test in my phone."

Briana starting scrolling through the pictures in her phone. She found the one of the pregnancy test. Briana lifted the phone so Bryan could see the picture.

"She said she is keeping it."

Bryan stood still and silent.

Briana's tears started to fall.

"Bri please listen."

"To what?"

"To me."

"So you can tell me more lies?"

"No Briana so that I can explain."

"I don't want to hear your explanation. I am sick and tired of your bullshit and your lies Bryan. And to think I actually contemplated coming back to be a family with you and the twins.

But you had to rip this family apart with this shit. I can't say that I hate you right now, but what I feel is pretty close to it."

She turned away but then turned back to face him.

"I love the twins but I am going to ask that you stay the fuck out of my life."

"Bri…"

Bryan walked closer to Briana. She backed up and wiped the tears from falling. She headed towards the front door.

"Baby please…"

Briana kept walking, so Bryan bolted to the front door to block it so Briana couldn't leave. Bryan kept pleading for Briana to listen to him as he stood blocking the door.

"Briana please give me a chance."

"No Bryan move."

"No Bri stop being so mean and listen to me."

Briana didn't respond she turned and headed towards the back door.

Bryan moved swiftly and grabbed Briana's arm snatching her back to him. He slammed her against the wall aggressively. Briana's eyes bulged in horror when her back hit the wall. She knew the other Bryan was still in there and would show up at any time.

"Bri I love you and I can't lose you." Bryan said in tears.

"Get off me!" Briana yelled.

She was trying to get away but Bryan had her pinned. They were sort of scuffling up against the wall.

"I can't lose you Bri" Brian said through his tears.

Daisia and Dalila heard the commotion and ran upstairs.

They had been ear hustling the whole time.

"Daddy let go stop it!" The twins yelled running towards Briana and Bryan.

The twins started grabbing their dad's arms. They began to cry. He was crying and struggling to grab at Briana to try and stop her from getting way.

"Bri I never meant to hurt you." He sobbed.

"Daddy! Stop!" The twins screamed.

"I never meant to hurt you."

He grabbed Briana's shirt and it ripped, so he grabbed her pants and it caused her to fall.

One of the twins ran to her.

"Bri!" The twin screamed with tears in her eyes.

"Bri please I need you!"

The other twin started screaming and crying "Daddy let her go!"

Bryan finally let go of Bri. He was so lost in his emotions he hadn't realized the scene that he created. He backed up from Briana and looked at the twins. Bryan walked slowly to the couch and sat down. He put his head in his hands and continued to cry.

Briana stood up, adjusted her clothes, and wiped her tears. Daisia hugged Briana tightly. Briana kissed her on the cheek and said. "I love you guys, I am sorry." Briana wiped Daisia's tears with her fingers.

She looked over at Dalila who was by her father and said "I am sorry."

Dalila ran to Briana and hugged her. "You girls be good ok? And

Listen to your father. I will always love you."

Briana let go of the twins. She walked out of the back door. Never to look back.

****

Briana never meant for it to go down like that. She never wanted the twins to be involved in her and Bryan's domestic situations. She felt extremely bad about that whole scene. Briana tried hard to hide the truth about their daddy from them. She tried to hide the truth about Bryan from everybody.

Eventually what was in the dark had finally to come to the light. The stuff that Briana thought she was hiding everyone already knew. It was hard for Briana to walk away from Bryan, but the hardest thing for Briana to do was to walk away from the twins. She loved those girls with every inch of herself and it took so much out of her when she left.

Briana knew that she should have left his ass so long ago. When she thought about it she never understood why she stayed. Part of her wished that Bryan would change. Part of her got stuck on trying to change him. There were times that Briana felt like she was one foot out of the door, but then she would allow Bryan to pull her back in.

She knew that she couldn't wait around for Bryan to get it together. Meeting his side chick was the icing on the cake. But that last situation sealed the deal for her. She couldn't live like that. She knew then just like she knows now that she is a better woman than how Bryan was treating her. She knew that she deserved better than the shit that Bryan was giving her.

Briana walked from her kitchen into her living room with a picture of her and the twins in her hands. She dabbed the tear falling from her eye with the Kleenex that she had in her hand. She prayed over the picture that they would grow up to be beautiful young women. She placed the picture in a small box she had sitting in the middle of the living room floor. The box was filled with old memories of her, Bryan, and the twins.

Briana picked up a T-shirt that Bryan bought her and placed it in the box. She sat down on the couch. She set the Kleenex she had in her hand on the table. She closed the box and put some tape on it. She took a deep breath and let it out slow. She was closing that chapter of her life and moving forward. There was no need to keep cluttering her life with all the stuff that kept her emotionally attached to Bryan and her life with him.

She said a prayer for Bryan and the twins and then stood up, picked up the box and walked out of the door to take the box to the trash. She walked across the parking lot at her apartment complex to the trash bins and threw the box in the trash.

She felt like a huge weight was lifted from her as soon as the box hit the bottom of the trash bin. She turned and walked back towards her apartment building with a smile on her face. It was time to call her girls and turn up.

Chapter 27

Briana

Moving Forward

That weekend Briana, Mercedes, and Imani met up at an Italian restaurant downtown Saint Paul. They were in the mood for a girl's night, so they decided food and drinks would be perfect.

Briana finally told her girls about Bryan over dinner. She revealed the whole truth, and she also told them about the situation that went down that night with the twins and Bryan. It had been a couple of months since the very last incident with Bryan so she felt comfortable with talking about it.

Imani was furious. Her face was deeply frowned as she stared and listened to Briana talk about the cheating and the fights.

Mercedes said. "I told you Imani."

Imani said. "Why didn't you ever tell us Bri?"

"I don't know. Part of me was embarrassed and part of me thought that he was going to change." Briana said and then picked up her glass of water and took a sip. The waiter walked up to bring them some more bread and butter.

"Thank you." Briana said to the waiter. The waiter walked away to help another table.

"His sick ass. He needs to be in jail!" Imani spat still talking about Bryan.

"He's a bitch ass nigga for real." Mercedes said.

Imani picked up a slice of the warm bread and a knife and began to spread butter on the bread. Her face was still frowned.

Briana grabbed a piece of the warm bread and took a bite.

"It's crazy when I think about all of it. I can't believe how lost I was in it."

"See ya'll should've let me beat his ass in the club that night on my birthday." Mercedes said.

She took a sip of her patron and pineapple.

"Mercedes you're a woman." Briana said looking at Mercedes take another sip of her drink

"You're right I was too cute that night. But I sure would a popped his ass right in the mouth and then let my goons beat his ass."

Briana chuckled a little bit with tears in her eyes.

"You should've called the police B…. I am so mad." Imani said.

"No need to be mad Imani. I'm the one who stayed in it." Briana said.

"Imma shoot his mutha fuckin house up." Mercedes said.

Just like Briana thought. Imani would want to call the police and Mercedes would want to go H.A.M (Hard as A MuthaFucka). She was in a better place now so it was easier for her to deal with their reactions. She was glad that her girls love her like they do. She needed the support from them while she was healing.

"Please don't Mercedes." Briana said.

Mercedes frowned.

Imani said. "We just love you girl and we got your back no matter what."

Briana Smiled and said "I love you guys too."

They squeezed hands around the table.

The waiter came back with their food. Mercedes ordered Fettuccini Alfredo. Imani ordered Shrimp linguine. Briana ordered vegetarian lasagna with a side order of spinach and artichoke bruschetta.

"Damn that's a lot of food Briana." Mercedes said.

"Shut up bitch I am hungry." Briana laughed and then Imani laughed.

Mercedes nudged Briana in the shoulder and started laughing with them.

Chapter 28

Briana

What The Future Holds

As she sat in a beach chair under an umbrella, she watched a young couple splash in the ocean water playing. She smiled and then turned her attention to the rest of the busy beach.

People were everywhere on the beach. There were a bunch of people in the water enjoying the ocean. Some were laying out sun bathing. Others were walking up and down the beach showing off their beautiful beach bodies.

She adjusted her shades and took a sip of her fruit drink. South Beach Miami, Florida was just what she needed right now. A half of year has gone by since the last time she had seen or talked to Bryan and the twins. Since the last altercation involving the twins, she focused her attention on work. Work and spending time with Imani and Mercedes kept her mind off of Bryan and the twins.

She closed her eyes she allowed herself to zone out on the sound of the water and the people around her talking and laughing. She put her hand on her protruding belly. She felt the baby move inside of her.

He reached out and touched her belly. "Are you ok B?" He asked.

Briana looked over at Malik relaxing in the beach chair next to hers. His shirt was off and his muscular chocolate chest and abs were exposed. He had on black, white and grey stripped beach shorts.

Briana's cute baby pink two piece and cover up showed off her baby bump. The cover up was a netted material that opened in the front. It was kind of a short sleeve, knee length jacket type of cover up. It was loose fitted, and hung like a robe on her body.

Briana nodded her head up and down. Then she said.

"Yes, the baby was moving."

Malik stood up and took a couple of steps towards Briana. He put both of his hands on her belly and began rubbing her belly.

"How does that feel?"

Briana smiled at Malik.

"Good."

Malik smiled and kissed her pregnant belly. He lifted up from kissing her belly to kiss her on the lips.

"You are so beautiful Queen." Malik said after he kissed her.

"Thank you King." Briana responded.

"I love you and I will be the man you deserve Briana." Malik was staring into Briana's eyes.

Since the last situation with Bryan, Malik and Briana had been spending more time with each other. He too contributed in Briana's healing by keeping her mind off of Bryan. They would go for walks around the lake after work until it got too cold outside for walks. Then they started going to the theater to see movies, or just chilling out at each other's house watching movies or just talking. They enjoyed each other and decided to take the trip together to Florida. Malik had become one of Briana's best friends.

Malik pulled a small black box out of his beach shorts pocket and handed it to Briana. He kneeled on one knee. Briana's eyes welled up with tears as she opened the box. A beautiful diamond ring was inside.

"Malik…." Briana said with a tear falling from her eye.

Malik said. "Will you be my wife?"

Briana replied. "Yes Malik I will be your wife."

They hugged each other. Malik wiped the tears from her eyes and cheeks. He removed the ring from the black box. Briana held her left hand out and watched Malik place the beautiful diamond ring on her ring finger. They hugged again. Malik leaned back down to kiss her pregnant belly. He looked up at her.

"I love you Briana Patrice Taylor."

Briana wiped her eyes again.

"I love you too Malik Jahlil Freeman."

Malik stood up.

"Ready to go in?" Malik asked.

"Yes I am." Briana said

Malik began to gather up their things so that they could head back to their hotel room.

Briana was so surprised. She wasn't expecting a proposal when they planned the trip. She thought they were coming to just to get out of Minnesota for a weekend.

She didn't know that Malik had hooked up with Imani and Mercedes to pick out the ring weeks before they took the trip down there. She didn't know that he had invited Imani and Mercedes down to Miami to celebrate with them. She didn't know that Imani and Mercedes were waiting back at the hotel room to surprise her.

She stared at her ring. After everything she had been through she deserved to be happy and at this moment she truly was. Malik had been nothing but a true friend to her through all of the ups and downs with Bryan. While they allowed their friendship to develop their love grew stronger for each other. Malik respected her and adorned her with his love, and Briana appreciated it.

Briana was able to let everything go without looking back. She let go of Bryan and the twins. She let go of the love she felt for Bryan, and she released the emotional attachment she had with him. Closing that door and that chapter of her life allowed better things to happen. Briana realized that the sun does shine again after the storm. She decided to keep her mind focused on the future and to keep moving forward. She vowed to herself and God that she was never going back.